"Profoundly moving and deeply human, this story of self-discovery and forgiveness is essential reading. I loved every word."

—BONNIE GARMUS, *New York Times* bestselling
author of *Lessons in Chemistry*

"I was enthralled from the first page of this short, powerful book. Maureen is a wonderful, frustrating character—so rigid, and so frightened of what she might learn about herself and her own past. We all have some Maureen inside us, and so the journey we take with her across England and into her own personal tumult is a satisfying, visceral one."

—ANN NAPOLITANO, *New York Times* bestselling
author of *Dear Edward*

"This book is a perfect gem. Fans of Olive Kitteridge and Eleanor Oliphant will love Maureen Fry, and it's a brilliant coda to the Harold Fry series."

—J. RYAN STRADAL, bestselling author of
The Lager Queen of Minnesota

"This is a quiet miracle of a book. I loved the absurdity of some scenes and the tenderness of others, and then I was met with the kind of gasp-able (truly—I gasped!) transcendent experience that only the best books can deliver. Rachel Joyce has been a favorite of mine since *The Unlikely Pilgrimage of Harold Fry,* and *Maureen* only reinforces my idea that she is a master at mixing humor and pathos, and at showing hard truths about life and living that nonetheless make us grateful to be here."

—ELIZABETH BERG, author of *The Story of Arthur Truluv* and *Earth's the Right Place for Love*

"I adored Harold and Queenie, but who knew Maureen waited in the wings to steal my heart? A testament to just how exquisitely Rachel Joyce understands people, and written with kindness and such perception. I can't recommend it enough."

—JOANNA CANNON, bestselling author of *The Trouble with Goats and Sheep* and *A Tidy Ending*

"Rachel Joyce has a genius for creating the most damaged and difficult characters and making us care deeply about their redemption. *Maureen* is a powerful finale to her classic trilogy of heartbreak and healing."

—CLARE CHAMBERS, author of *Small Pleasures*

"At last it's Maureen's turn! It may only have the physical heft of a novella but Rachel Joyce's angry-sad latest packs the weight of a long marriage into the space of several well-ironed handkerchiefs. Just brilliant."

—PATRICK GALE, author of *Take Nothing With You* and *A Place Called Winter*

"Maureen is so beautifully and unflinchingly portrayed—a complex contradiction of brittle and prickly with an underbelly of fragility and fear. Her journey, both physical and psychological, is compelling and profoundly moving and leaves the reader feeling fully satisfied and just a little lighter."

—RUTH HOGAN, author of *Madame Burova* and *The Keeper of Lost Things*

"Rachel Joyce is deeply attuned to the complex rhythms of life and love and she sublimates this understanding, sentence by delicate, powerful, glistening sentence, into an unforgettable story. It's beautiful all through, but the closing chapters are just astonishing, transcendent and hope-filled and life-affirming. I'll never forget this wonderful novel or the sunny, slightly teary day I spent reading it."

—DONAL RYAN, author of *The Queen of Dirt Island* and *Strange Flowers*

"Beautifully written and endlessly touching, Rachel Joyce once again captures what it means to be human in the final book of her wonderful trilogy."

—PHAEDRA PATRICK, author of *The Book Share* and *The Library of Lost and Found*

"This book is short but very special. As fans of Rachel Joyce might expect, it's funny, touching and quite beautiful. It's also packed with wisdom about love and loss—and is sure to provide comfort to anyone who's known grief."

—MATT CAIN, author of *The Secret Life of Albert Entwistle*

"In this slender, lyrical novel, Rachel Joyce offers a story as epic and encompassing as that wide-armed Angel of the North. A journey of redemption, forgiveness and love. A journey you don't want to miss."

—HELEN PARIS, author of *Lost Property*

"Maureen is the sort of person we pass in the street every day, every hour, and probably give little thought to. She is difficult, perhaps, a little brittle, unable to engage successfully with the world, and maybe hard to warm to—an embattled figure often lost against the vast opera of life. But Rachel allows us to see into her complex universe, feel firsthand her fears, the profound longing, the grim phantoms of the past, the ordered rebelliousness, and strange, dark sense of humor—and of shame. This story also happens to tie three life-affirming, vital, and unpredictable novels together into a perfect, never-ending dance."

—DAMIAN DIBBEN, author of *The Color Storm*

"Rachel Joyce writes with incredible depth, beauty and heart. Reading her prose is like listening to great music—sometimes soft and sweet, sometimes heart-rending, always beguiling. This is an emotional story about loss, resilience and reconciliation. Maureen Fry is a prickly kind of star . . . but wow, how she shines!"

—HAZEL PRIOR, author of *Call of the Penguins*

"This is a deceptively simple story of love, forgiveness, fulfilment and hope. I can't think of any other novelist quite as tender and compassionate as Rachel Joyce, who understands that miracle of transformation when human fragility becomes strength of spirit."

—BEL MOONEY, author of *Lifelines*

"This is a fitting and deeply moving end to the trilogy of Harold Fry. A portrait of a woman adrift in grief, it is as fragile as a songbird and just as beautiful."

—SARAH WINMAN, author of *Still Life*

PRAISE FOR THE HAROLD FRY TRILOGY

"A gentle adventure with an emotional wallop."

—*USA Today*

"A cause for celebration."

—*The Washington Post*

"Beguiling . . . [A] modest-seeming story that . . . enthralls and moves you as it unfolds."

—*People*

"Gorgeously poignant."

—*O: The Oprah Magazine*

"Funny, tender and with a heart-stopping twist to boot."

—*New Zealand Woman's Weekly*

"Rachel Joyce probes questions that are as simple as they are profound: Can we begin to live again, and live truly, as ourselves, even in middle age, when all seems ruined? Can we believe in hope when hope seems to have abandoned us? I found myself laughing through tears."

—PAULA McLAIN, *New York Times* bestselling author of *The Paris Wife*

"This funny, poignant story moved and inspired me."

—NANCY HORAN, *New York Times* bestselling author of *Loving Frank*

"Marvelous!"

—HELEN SIMONSON, *New York Times* bestselling author of *Major Pettigrew's Last Stand*

BY RACHEL JOYCE

MAUREEN

MAUREEN

A Harold Fry Novel

Rachel Joyce

THE DIAL PRESS

NEW YORK

A Dial Press Trade Paperback Original

Copyright © 2022 by Rachel Joyce
Book club guide copyright © 2023 by Penguin Random House LLC

Published in the United States by The Dial Press, an imprint of Random House, a division of Penguin Random House LLC, New York.

THE DIAL PRESS is a registered trademark and the colophon is a trademark of Penguin Random House LLC.
RANDOM HOUSE BOOK CLUB and colophon are trademarks of Penguin Random House LLC.

Originally published in hardcover in the United Kingdom as *Maureen Fry and the Angel of the North* by Doubleday, an imprint of Transworld Publishers, a division of Penguin Random House UK, in 2022.

The interview comes from an original recording for BBC Radio 4's Bookclub program, presented by James Naughtie and recorded in 2021. Used by permission.

ISBN 978-0-593-44642-3
Ebook ISBN 978-0-593-44643-0

Printed in the United States of America on acid-free paper

Illustrations by Andrew Davidson

randomhousebooks.com
randomhousebookclub.com

2 4 6 8 9 7 5 3 1

Book design by Caroline Cunningham

For Susanna

The corpse you planted last year in your garden,

Has it begun to sprout? Will it bloom this year?

The Waste Land, T. S. Eliot

I thought I saw an angel in an azure robe coming towards me across the lawn, but it was only the blue sky through the feathering branches of the lime.

Kilvert's Diary, July 21, 1873

OPENING STICKY CLOSET DOORS

We have a closet door that is always sticking. It's the kind of closet where we shove in things that we don't want to deal with, but can't yet throw out. And part of the deal with the stickiness of this door is that you know its difficulty will make it even easier to keep closed and ignore what's behind. To me, writing is about opening those kinds of sticky doors. The kind of doors your characters will do everything they can to convince you are not there. Closed closets, complete with wallpaper over the top.

More than ten years ago, Harold Fry stepped into my imagination and transformed my world. He had been around me since my father's death. Writing about his journey to save his dying friend in *The Unlikely Pilgrimage of Harold Fry* helped me in some way to bear my own grief. He also helped me fulfill my deeply held longing to finish writing a book that someone might consider for publication. I have a lot to thank Harold for. And after that, he made his way, without me, into the minds of other people, who read his story and met him within their own imaginations. There were crazy times. Whistle-stop book tours that took me all over the world, including China. One day twenty Spanish journalists pitched up outside our house. But there were many quiet meetings, too. I am thinking now of a man I was introduced to who was staying in a shelter for the homeless where the book had been available as a free gift. This man warmly told me it was the best book he'd ever read. This was quickly qualified as being the only book he'd read. Followed by the fact that he hadn't read it because he couldn't. Other people from the shelter had told him the story, chapter by chapter, as he held the book in his hands. That was a gift. For me, I mean. When someone is so generous as to tell you why your story means something to them, it is as close as I come to understanding why I keep doing it. Why I keep trying to find the moment where the ordinary spills outward and acquires a more numinous quality, like a kind of halo.

When the book was first published, another reader, a very well-read woman this time, came up to me at a book-signing and said, "You do know this is a trilogy?" (Actually, what she said was, "You do know this is a *triptych*?") In some ways, this was music to my ears. I was missing the characters so much, I felt sort of bereaved all over again. And I could see there were characters who had not been fully realized in Harold's story because they could not be. But I also knew that I had no intention of doing what she was asking me to do. She pointed out that as far as Maureen—Harold's difficult wife—was concerned, there was still, in effect, a closet door I had left closed. But the problem was that I shared Maureen's point of view. I didn't wish to open it. I wasn't ready to face what Maureen has to face. I write about characters with a complexity I recognize I need to know better, but Maureen was a step too far.

What I *did* do was tackle the second book. I wrote *The Love Song of Miss Queenie Hennessy* as a companion story, neither a sequel nor a prequel, but a free-standing novel you might read without having picked up the first one, or that you could—if you so desired—read side by side with Harold, finding little juxtapositions and echoes along the way. I had spoken a lot about Queenie when doing book events and signings, and it seemed right to give her a voice. Not just her back story—the story of how she came to be working in a brewery as an accountant in the first place. (Queenie was not a properly trained accountant, I always knew that.) There was the story of her friendship with David and how her unexpressed love for Harold drove her to a compromised place with his son. There was the story, too, of what happened to her after she left Harold. But the books and characters that interest me are those that challenge my own way of thinking—and here was an invitation to explore the world of the hospice where Queenie was dying, a world which had frightened my father when he was dying, and consequently frightened me, too.

So there. Queenie had been brought into the open. I had faced my own insecurities and misconceptions about the hospice. After that, I happily got on with other books, other characters, other questions and ideas.

But I left Maureen's closet door closed.

And, mostly, I would say I got away with it.

Except I knew I hadn't.

Then came the COVID-19 pandemic and, with it, lockdown. We all experienced what Maureen experiences when Harold begins his walk to Queenie: that sense of existing within the confines of the same four walls, that strange disabling of time and boundaries that occurs when routine is taken away and you are left alone with yourself. And I thought a lot about Maureen. I thought how grief and loss can become our identity, one that can keep us out on our own, not with the dead but not with the living either. I thought about how hard it is to move on without feeling deep down that you have betrayed the person you have lost. I thought about my own relationship with my father, and how, even fifteen years after his death, I had never really allowed myself to say goodbye. I realized I was ready to try to help Maureen make that difficult journey of reconciliation that she needs to make, alone and apart from Harold. I thought, if these characters are still so strongly in my mind, then why not write about them?

So here we pick up Harold and Maureen in 2022, ten years after the walk that changed Harold's life, and Maureen's, too. They have lived through the pandemic. Harold is at ease with himself. The walk has brought him a kind of peace. He and Maureen had been living in a kind of cold void, unable to talk about the terrible loss that left them estranged, and now they are able to reconnect. But even though their marriage has been healed by his walk, Maureen knows that something inside her still has not healed. She has not been *out*. She has not made that solitary journey into the unfamiliar. Besides, I felt I had set something up with Harold's pilgrimage—something about the kindness, the *beauty* of strangers, I suppose—that I needed to test. To see if it was the same ten years later, given how much the world has changed. And the result is this book.

So my reader was right (as readers generally are). It was a trilogy, after all, and maybe even a triptych. This is the end of the journey for me and Harold and his wife, Maureen, and his old friend, Queenie, and it is the end, too, of the tragedy of the young man they loved, all three of them. The closets have been opened and we have looked at what was inside, and let it go. It was not so daunting, after all.

The moment I handed in the final draft of this book, I went into the garden and something happened. I saw—in the shadows of my imagination—a new set of characters, a new set of questions. It was as if they had been politely standing out of view for a long time, each with a suitcase—which is a kind of portable closet, after all—ready to talk to me as soon as I was ready.

So I kept gardening and I began to listen as new doors opened.

JUNE 2022

MAUREEN

WINTER JOURNEY

It was too early for birdsong. Harold lay beside her, his hands neat on his chest, looking so peaceful she wondered where he traveled in his sleep. Certainly not the places she went: if she closed her eyes, she saw roadworks. Dear God, she thought. This is no good. She got up in the pitch-black, took off her nightdress and put on her best blue blouse with a pair of comfortable slacks and a cardigan. "Harold?" she called. "Are you awake?" But he didn't stir. She picked up her shoes and shut the bedroom door without a sound. If she didn't go now, she never would.

Downstairs she switched on the kettle, and while it boiled, she got out her Marigolds and wiped a few surfaces. "Maureen," she said out loud, because she was no fool. She could tell what she was doing, even if her hands couldn't. Fussing, that's what. She made a flask of instant coffee and a round of sandwiches that she wrapped in clingfilm, then wrote him a message. She wrote another that said "Mugs!" and another that said "Pans!" and before she knew it, the kitchen was covered with Post-it notes, like small yellow alarm signals. "Maureen," she said again, and took them all down. "Go now. Go." She hung Harold's wooden cane from the chair where he couldn't miss it, then slipped the Thermos into her bag along with the sandwiches, put on her driving shoes and winter coat, picked up her suitcase and stepped out into the beautiful early morning. The sky was clear and pointed with stars, and the moon was like the white part of a fingernail. The only light came from Rex's house next door. And still no birdsong.

It was cold, even for January. The crazy paving had frozen overnight and she had to grab hold of the handrail. There were splinters of ice in the ruts between stones, and the front garden was no more than a few glass thorns. She turned on the ignition to warm the car while she scraped at the windows. The frost was rough, like sandpaper, and lay as far as she could see, slick beneath the street lamps of Fossebridge Road, but no one else was out. It was a Sunday, after all. She waved at Rex's house in case he was awake, and that was it. She was going.

Road-gritters had already passed through Fore Street, and salt lay in pink mats all the way up the hill. She drove north past the bookstore and the other shops that would be closed until Monday, but she didn't look. It was a good while since she'd used the high street. These days, she and Harold mostly went online, and not just because of the pandemic. The quiet row of shops became night-lit rows of houses. In turn they became a dark emptiness with a closed-down petrol station somewhere in the middle. She passed the turning for the crematorium that she visited once a month and kept driving. Now that she was on the road, she felt not excitement, but more a sense that, even though she didn't know how to explain it, she was doing the right thing. Harold had been right.

"You have to go, Maureen," he'd said. She had come up with a list of reasons why she couldn't but in the end she'd agreed. She'd offered to show him how to use the dishwasher and the washing machine because he sometimes got confused about which buttons to press and then she wrote the instructions clearly on a piece of paper.

"You are sure?" she'd said again, a few days later. "You really think I should do this?"

"Of course I'm sure." He was sitting in the garden while she raked old leaves. He'd done up his coat lopsided, so that the left half of him was adrift from the right.

"But who will take care of you?"

"I will take care of me."

"What about meals? You need to eat."

"Rex can help."

"That's no good. Rex is worse than you are."

"That is true, of course. Two old fools!"

At this, he'd smiled. Only, something about the completeness of his smile made her miss him without even going anywhere, so that he could be as sure as he damn well liked, but she wasn't. She had put down her rake. Gone to him and redid his buttons. He sat patiently, gazing up at her with his delft-blue eyes. No one but Harold had ever looked at her like that.

She stroked his hair and then he lifted his fingertips to her face, and drew her down to his, and kissed her.

"Maureen, you won't feel right unless you go," he'd said.

"Okay, then. I'm going. I'm going, and nothing will stop me! Though, if you don't mind, I won't walk. I'll take the more conventional route, thank you very much. I'll drive."

They'd laughed because they both knew she was doing her best to sound bigger than she felt. After that she went back to raking the leaves and he went back to watching the sky, but the silence was filled with all the things she did not know how to say.

So here she was, with Harold in her head, while she traveled further and further away from him. Only last night he had cleaned her driving shoes and set them, side by side, next to the chair with her clothes. "I won't wake you in the morning," she'd promised, as they got into bed and said good night. He had held his hand tight round hers until he fell asleep, and then she had curled up close and listened to the steady repeat of his heart, trying to take in some of his peacefulness.

Maureen drove slowly but there was hardly any traffic. If a car came toward her with its headlights shining, she saw it in plenty of time and pulled over in the right place—she even waved a polite thank-you—then the lanes were dark again, just the swing of hedge and tree as she passed. From there, she joined a dual carriageway and that was even better because the road was straight and wide and still pretty empty, with lorries parked in lay-bys. But as she got closer to Exeter, there were lots of roadworks, exactly as she'd dreamed during the night, and she got confused by the detours. She was no longer on the

A38, but instead a chain of bypasses and residential roads, with many mini-roundabouts in between. Maureen drove for another twenty minutes before it occurred to her that the yellow diversion signs had stopped a while back and she had come to the edge of a housing estate. All she could see were blocks of flats and bony trees growing in spaces between paving slabs. It was still dark.

"Oh, well, that's great," she said. "That's marvelous." It wasn't just herself she spoke to. She also had a habit of talking to the silence as if it were deliberately making things difficult for her. Increasingly she could not tell the difference between what she thought and what she said.

Maureen passed more flats and more tiny trees and cars parked everywhere, as well as delivery vans on the early shift, but still no sign of the A38. She turned down a long service road because there was a row of bright street lamps in the distance, only to find herself at the bottom of a dead end, with a large depot to her left that was surrounded by a set of open gates and spiked fencing.

She pulled over and got out her road map but she had no idea where to start looking. She turned on her mobile but that was no use either, and anyway Harold would still be asleep. For a moment she just sat there. Already confounded. Harold would say, "Ask someone," but that was Harold. The whole point of driving was that she wouldn't have to deal with people she didn't know. "Okay," she said firmly. "You can do this." She would take her map and be like Harold. She would ask for help at the depot.

Maureen got out of the car, and at once she felt the cold

against her face and ears and inside her nose. As she crossed the car park, security lamps snapped on to her left and right, almost blinding her. She could make out light from a prefab cabin to the left of the main building but she had to go cautiously, with her arms shot out to keep her balance. Maureen's driving shoes were those flat suede ones with a bar across the top and special gripper soles; they were good on wet pavements but nothing was good on black ice. There were notices with pictures of dogs, warning that the premises were regularly patrolled, and she was afraid they might come running out. When she was a child, the local farmer had let his dogs roam freely. She still had a little scar beneath her chin.

Maureen rapped at the window of the hut. The young man on night duty wasn't even awake. He was hunched in a fold-out camping chair, the turban on his head crushed against the wall, his mouth agape and his legs sprawled all over the place. She knocked again, a bit louder, and called, "Excuse me!"

He rubbed his eyes, startled. He pulled himself out of his chair and seemed to grow and grow. He was so tall he had to duck as he stumbled to the window, putting on his mask only as an afterthought. He had a thick brown beard, with hefty shoulders like a boxer's, and his hands were so large he had a problem undoing the catch on the window. He slid it open and crooked his neck sideways as he blinked and stared down at her.

"I'm not going to pretend. I'm lost. I'm trying to get to the M5 but all those roadworks on the A38 sent me off in the wrong direction." Her voice was louder than she'd intended because of the window, which she had to reach up toward, but also because she was anxious and he might not understand.

Besides, she hated admitting she'd made a mistake. It wasn't as if she didn't know the route.

He gazed at her another moment, trying his best to wake up. Then he said, "You're lost?"

"It was the roadworks. Normally I'm fine. Normally I have no problem. I just need to get to the M5." She was doing it again. She was shouting.

He moved away from the window and opened the door at the side. She waited, not knowing what he expected her to do, just worrying about those dogs, until he called, "Excuse me?" So she put on her mask and went round.

Now that she was in the cabin, the young man seemed even larger. The top of her head would barely reach his chest. He stood with his neck at an angle and his body hunched to make it smaller. Even his shoes—a pair of solid black lace-ups, the kind they used to put on children to correct their feet—couldn't get enough space. And it was obvious why he'd been asleep. An old electric fire blazed out orange heat from beneath the window. It was like being spit-roasted from the ankles upward. Anyone would have fallen asleep next to that. Maureen swallowed a yawn.

He said, "You don't want to go shouting at random strangers that you're lost. It's not safe. They might take advantage of you."

His English was perfect. If anything he had a Devon accent. So there you were. That was another thing she'd been completely wrong about. "I don't think anyone would want to take advantage of me."

"You never know. There are all sorts of people in the world."

"You are right, of course. But can you help me or not?"

"Yeah. Okay. I think so." He tip-tapped a few things into his phone and held it out for her. It was no use: it was a map but tiny. He showed her where she was and all the roads she needed to take to get to the M5. "See?"

"No," she said. "I don't. I don't see. That makes no sense to me."

"Why not?"

"I don't know. It just doesn't."

"Do you have a GPS?"

"We do have a GPS but I don't use it."

He seemed confused but she wasn't going to enlighten him. The fact was she'd had the GPS disconnected. She couldn't bear that nice voice urging directions at her and telling her last minute that she'd missed the turn. Maureen was of the generation who had grown up with the phone on the hall table, and a map in the glove compartment. Even online shopping was a stretch. Twenty lemons instead of two, and all that kind of thing.

He said, "Will you remember if I tell you?"

"I don't think I will."

"I don't know what to do, then. What do you want me to do?"

"I would like you to read out the directions from your phone and I will write them down on a piece of paper. I'll take my route from that."

"Oh, okay," he said. He touched his beard and realigned his feet, as if this was going to take a whole different kind of posture in order to make it work. "I see. Okay."

Patiently, he told her to go to the end of the road, turn left, take a right, the second exit at the roundabout, and she wrote it all down on a page he had torn from a notebook. He paused at the end of each new instruction, to make sure she'd written it down. By the end she had twelve in all, and every one of them numbered.

"Do you know where you're heading after that?"

"Yes." She pointed at the place on her road map.

"That's a very long way."

"I know."

"At least you'll get a change of scene."

"I'm not looking for a change of scene. All I want is to get there."

"Do you know your way after the M5?"

"Yes."

"The junction numbers?"

"I think so."

He looked at her for a moment, without saying anything. She got the feeling he didn't believe her. Then he said, "Why don't you write those down, too? You don't want to get lost on a motorway."

He pulled his phone close to his face as he squinted a little and slowly read out the motorway exits she needed, plus the directions from there. There was no irritation in his voice. If anything, he seemed worried that he might get one of them wrong and mislead her. He shook his head as if he couldn't believe she was going to drive all that distance by herself, and in one day. "It's so far," he kept saying.

"Thank you," she told him, once he finished. "And I'm sorry if I woke you."

"That's okay. I shouldn't be asleep."

She thought he might be smiling behind his mask, so she smiled too. "You've been kind."

"Huh." He shoved his hands into his pockets and turned to gaze out of the window. She was still on one side of the cabin and he was on the other, but their reflections were caught against the dark outside, like two see-through people, he so big, and she so short and trim, with her cap of white hair. "That's not what most people call me."

It came out of the blue. An honesty she didn't expect. She would have liked to be able to say something to make him feel better—she would have liked to be that kind of person, if only so that she could get back into her car and drive on with his instructions, without feeling she had failed. But she couldn't. She couldn't find it. That fleeting moment of goodness. People imagined they might reach each other, but it wasn't true. No one understood another's grief or another's joy. People were not see-through at all.

Maureen pursed her mouth. The young man gazed sadly at something or nothing in the dark. The silence seemed to go on and on. She looked at the floor and took in his black lace-ups again. They were such earnest shoes, like someone trying really hard.

"Well," he said, "I guess you should be okay now."

"Yes," she said.

"What's your name?"

"Mrs. Fry."

"I'm Lenny."

"Goodbye, Lenny."

"It was nice to meet you, Mrs. Fry. Just don't go shouting at people that you're lost. And drive carefully. It's cold out there."

"I'm going to see our son," she said. Then she left and got into the car and made a U-turn to get back to the road.

2

THE WORLD'S GUEST

Ten years ago, Harold had gone into the world without Maureen. He had left to post a letter to his dying friend Queenie and, on the spur of the moment, made up his mind to walk the 627 miles to her instead. He had met many people along the way. Given up his wallet and slept in the wild. The story even hit the news and briefly made him famous. Left behind, Maureen had gone on a journey, too, but hers wasn't the kind people talked about or bought postcards of to send home. She *was* at home. That was the whole point. Harold was walking the length of England to save a woman he had worked with once, while Maureen cleaned the kitchen sink. And when she had finished cleaning the sink, she was upstairs, squirting circles of polish at his bedroom furniture. Keeping herself as busy as possible when there was absolutely nothing left to do.

She was even washing things she had already washed, just to find a little more washing inside them. And there were also days—though, again, who had known about them but her?—when she couldn't think how to get up in the morning. When she crawled out of bed and stared for hours at the laundry and the sink, and asked what was the point in washing or scrubbing when it made not one shred of difference? She was so alone she didn't know where to look or what to think about. She wasn't even sure that Harold would come home. The panic that had engulfed her was unfamiliar and frightening.

But that was in the past. Maureen didn't like to talk about that time any more. She knew it would sound sad, and it wasn't. There were far worse things. Harold had finished his walk to Queenie. Maureen had traveled to be with him when Queenie died. Together they had returned home and started again. Maureen nursed him slowly back to health, cooking all those dishes he loved when they were first married, bandaging the blisters and welts on his feet that no one else knew about. It was true they were somewhat shy of one another in bed to begin with because they had grown so used to sleeping apart, and she could still recall the bashfulness with which he had first called her "sweetheart" as if she might laugh in his face. But she didn't. She liked it very much. They had taken daily strolls to the quay and he listened to her ideas for making new vegetable beds and redecorating the house. Sometimes people stopped to shake his hand because they had heard what he'd done, and she would wait, slightly to the side, not quite know-ing how to set her face, not even quite knowing what to do with her hands, both proud and bewildered by how at ease with himself he had become. Now he was seventy-five and she was seventy-two: their marriage had arrived at a good new place, like their very own private creek. Once in a while, Harold received a card from one of the women he had walked with—Kate—but Maureen put it out of her mind and they got on with their lives. Then, five months ago, there had been more news about Queenie. The woman was back in their lives all over again.

Light was coming. Lenny's instructions worked perfectly. Maureen found her way back to the A38, and drove past barrow-shaped earthworks to merge with the M5. In the east there was a darkness that wasn't entirely dark, and the navy-blue horizon was rimmed with pink and gold, while Venus still hung high and bright. Shapes came seeping back to life. Scribbled outlines of trees. Black shadows she guessed were pylons. More depots and warehouses. A lifeless hump at the roadside that might be a badger or a muntjac. Ice patches along the roadside held reflections of the new light, like pieces of stained glass, but beyond them, the land was still flat and dimmed and empty. Maureen pictured Harold fast asleep at home. Later he would pad down to the kitchen in his bare feet, the way he did every morning, and open the back door to look at the sky. Hours he could spend, doing nothing but gazing upward. He didn't even wear his watch. He preferred not knowing the time. On a good day he took his wooden cane because his legs were so weak he couldn't get to the end of the road any more, let alone the quay, and he watered the vegetable beds, entranced by the silver arc of water as it pooled over the earth, or he and Rex set up the drafts board and talked about this and that, but what he loved most was sitting on the patio, watching for birds. Whenever she felt a snatch of impatience, she told herself she was missing the point. At least he was happy, at least he was safe. And his health, too. At least he had that. It wasn't that he was losing his mind, rather that he was deliberately taking things out of it that he no longer needed.

Maureen indicated left and shifted to the nearside lane. The traffic was getting heavier. It made her anxious and she drove too slowly so that lorries came up behind with their headlights all blazing, and then went thundering past, churning up grit. Cullompton. Tiverton. The pin-sized silhouette of the Wellington Monument on the Blackdown Hills. Taunton. There had been a Slovak woman from Taunton who had been kind to Harold, but she'd got in touch a few years ago to say she was being deported. Harold had been very low about that. Rex asked local people to sign a petition, but it made no difference. And anyway he had three pages of signatures that all looked the same. "Bottom line, Mrs. Fry, the woman doesn't belong here," one neighbor told Maureen. Another said he wasn't racist and he had nothing against the person in question, but it was time to look after your own. That was back in the days, of course, when she wasn't ashamed to show her face on the high street.

The sun rose, blooming over the frozen land, turning everything the red of a geranium, even gulls and traffic. The moon was still out but no more than a chalk ghost, reluctant to commit either to staying or going. At Bridgwater she passed the giant Willow Man caught in the act of striding south with arms outstretched like long fins. Anti-vax slogans were sprayed on the concrete underside of a bridge. *Fake News. Fake Virus.* England was a different country from the one Harold had walked through. Sometimes he would tell a story about a person he had met back then, or a view across the hills, and she would listen as if she were watching a film with her eyes closed, unable to find the right pictures. These days it was all safe motorways and Uber. It was paying with your phone, and please keep your distance, not to mention podcasts, milk made of oats and meat made of plants, and everything streamed online. Look for a bank spilling with primroses and you'd more likely find an old blue mask caught in the leaves. Ten years ago she couldn't have imagined all the change that was coming.

Maureen switched on the radio but it was a news story about a film star who had staged a hate crime against himself to boost his Instagram profile. She turned it off. People expected so much of the world.

I want to be the world's guest.

The words took her by surprise. It was her son who had spoken them, but she hadn't thought of them in years. He must have been only six. He had looked straight up at her with his deep brown eyes that seemed to know a sadness she didn't.

"What on earth do you mean?" she had said.

"I don't know."

"Is it because you want a biscuit?"

"No."

"Then what is it you want? A party?"

"I don't like parties."

"Everyone likes parties."

"I don't. I don't like the games. I only like the cake and the going-home present."

"So what do you mean?"

"I don't know."

She had felt pierced. Everything about David had saddened her—his solemn gaze and his slow walk and the way he kept himself apart from other children. "Why don't you play?" she would say, when she took him to the park. "Those children look nice. I'm sure they'll play with you."

"It's okay, thank you," he would say. "I'll stay with you. I think they won't like me."

But she'd had the sense, even then, that he did know what he meant about being the world's guest. That he was just waiting for her to catch up. Forever she had been running after this child. Even now she was doing it.

Maureen felt dizzy suddenly. Almost seasick. She needed coffee and the washroom.

3

FRIED EGG

The waitress said it was okay for her to drink from her own flask but she would have to go to the counter and buy something to eat. Maureen asked if the waitress could take her order from the table because that was where she was already sitting, and the waitress said she couldn't. It was still early. The service station was empty, apart from Maureen and an old man whose hands trembled as he lifted his cup. Across from the Fresh Food Café, a woman in a hijab mopped the floor and another was opening the shutters on a shop.

"What difference does it make," said Maureen, "if you take my order here or at the counter? Show me the menu and I'll order something."

The waitress said there was no menu, not as such, and anyway it wasn't waitress service. She wore a baggy black top with a sequin rabbit on the front. Her finger ends were chewed and her hair was oily and colorless. The happiest thing about her was that rabbit.

"This is silly," said Maureen. "You're standing at my table. Why can't you take my order?"

"I'm cleaning it," said the waitress, and she gave it another antiseptic spray to prove her point. "I'm only allowed to serve you at the counter. It's the new regulations."

Maureen followed the waitress to the counter, but then she had to queue behind a family of five who had just arrived and were now ordering huge drinks from the coffee menu that had nothing to do with coffee. When it came to Maureen's turn, the waitress went through the breakfast options. It seemed to Maureen she was taking it slowly on purpose. There were pastries, muffins, iced doughnuts and sandwiches, as displayed beneath the counter. She pointed at each one. There was also a Full English, or a Gluten-free Vegan English, but those had to be done in the kitchen. There wasn't any more of the Winter Warmer Special because they had run out.

"If you don't have it, you should take it off the menu," said Maureen.

"So what do you want?"

Maureen told her she certainly didn't want the full breakfast. It would be too much. "I'll have an egg."

"Without the Full English?"

"Yes."

"Would you like the Full English to the side?"

"No," said Maureen. "I would like it not on my plate."

"Okay." The waitress picked up an iPad. "How would you like the egg?"

"Poached."

"We do fried."

"That's all?"

"Yes."

"If you only have fried, why did you ask how I'd like it?"

"People say fried."

"Seriously?" said Maureen.

"Seriously," said the waitress.

"Fine. I'll have fried."

"Toast?"

"Are you going to ask what kind and then tell me you only do white?"

A blush stung the waitress's neck and spread right up to her hairline. "No. We do brown. We also do ciabatta and gluten-free."

"I want brown. Not too thickly sliced. And toast it properly. I don't want warm bread. Butter to the side. I will butter it myself."

The waitress put something in her iPad that seemed to take much longer than "fried egg and toast," then gave Maureen a wooden spoon with a number on it and took her order through to the kitchen. Maureen went back to her table with the wooden spoon. Outside, six seagulls were sitting in the children's play area and a long strip of plastic tape flapped from the arms of a tree. Then, on the other side of the café, a woman of her own age arrived with someone younger who must be her daughter, pushing a buggy. She nodded at Maureen as if to say hello, and Maureen nodded back, but she didn't smile. The younger woman hoisted out a baby, and lifted her up, so that Maureen could see she was dressed in a padded pink snowsuit with a fur trim around the hood. It looked too hot, Maureen thought. The younger woman said she would get coffees if her mother held the baby and her mother said, "Sounds like a plan, Lou," and took the baby on her lap. Maureen watched the way she unzipped the pink snowsuit while her daughter wasn't looking and pulled down the hood. She watched the way the woman drew the baby's head to her mouth and kissed it and, without even being close, Maureen knew that bread-sweet smell of a baby's head and the downy softness of its hair. For a moment she allowed herself to pretend she was this woman with her grandchild, and she could feel the love falling right out of her. Then pain, a kind of envy, seemed to flood her entire body, like a dark messy injection of poison. It was everything she could do to keep still and bear it. So here she was. Back in the same old place. She thought she had dealt with the past but there were times recently, there were times even after thirty years, when she hated the world for taking away what she wanted most. If only she were able to be more like Harold. Letting things go, piece by piece.

"Table thirteen?" The waitress put the plate in front of her. She said, "Stay safe!"

Stay safe? Maureen wanted to ask. How exactly does that work? But instead she looked at the egg and said, "What is that?"

It was so hard it looked made of plastic. It looked like one of those comedy eggs you bought in a joke shop. And the bread was not toasted—it didn't even look warmed up—with butter not to the side, but splodged thickly all over the top. "No," she said. "You can't expect me to eat that."

The waitress lowered her head so that her oily hair hung forward, all in one piece. She made a sucky noise, like a string of hiccups.

"You need to take it away," said Maureen. "You can't charge me for that. I want my money back."

She poured another cup of coffee from her flask and unwrapped the clingfilm from her sandwiches and had those instead. The waitress pinched the plate away from Maureen as if she were dangerous, and took it back to the kitchen.

A short while later another woman came out. She walked straight to Maureen's table. She was twice the age of the waitress and her hair was cut in tufts that were dyed different shades of red, with pencilled eyebrows that didn't move.

"I hear you want your money back." She dropped a pile of loose change on the table, not even in pound coins but ones that no one used any more, like 5p pieces and pennies. She made no apology for the egg. Then she said, "I'm going to have to ask you to leave."

"I'm sorry?"

"You can't consume your own food and drink on the premises. There's a sign." She pointed to one at the entrance next to another that asked customers to respect social distancing and the wearing of masks, as well as being kind to staff at all times.

"But the waitress told me I could."

"You were rude."

"I didn't say anything."

"It's exactly that tone of voice I'm talking about. The poor girl is in tears because of you. If you want to eat your own food, you can do it outside."

Maureen was speechless. All she could do was sit there. The grandmother and her daughter turned their heads to watch what she would do next, and so did the man with trembling hands. "Are you really asking me to leave?" When it came, her voice was shaking and shrill. It was the spike in her. She'd always had it, even when she was a child. Parenthood had come to her mother and father late—too late to rekindle a marriage that had gone cold. Her father doted on her, and her mother—though she criticized her frequently—was determined that Maureen should have the life she had not.

"Oh, little Maureen," her father used to say, his eyes watery with pride. "There's nothing little Maureen can't do."

The woman with red hair was staring straight back at her. "Correct," she said. "I'm asking you to leave."

Maureen wiped her cup with a paper napkin and screwed it back on top of the flask, but her hands were shaking. She couldn't get the clingfilm to fit around what was left of her sandwiches, and when she tried to put on her coat, she kept missing the sleeve. As she left the service station, she thought of the grandmother gently cupping the baby's head and how she would never be one of those women. And she should never have told David that everyone liked parties: that was rot. She hated parties. She always had. You lied to children simply because their unhappiness was too much to bear.

Maureen picked her way across the car park feeling thin and

pinched. Exposed. As if all the goodness was behind her, while she was in the cold. She tried to tell herself it didn't matter but something solid was lodged in her throat like a bit of cheese she couldn't swallow. She would not give in. She would not weep. A seagull tore at a McDonald's bag with its beak, holding it down with its yellow webbed foot, then lifting into the air with a French fry. She wanted to ring Harold, but if she did, she would wake him and he would hear the distress in her voice and begin to worry. Then, out of nowhere, came an old memory of a shop of people—all swiveled round, staring, appalled—and another shrapnel of shame went right through her.

"Maureen," she said out loud. "Spilled milk, Maureen."

The grandmother would have eaten that fried egg. She would have smiled at the waitress and said, "Thank you, dear," and eaten every last plasticky scrap.

Another three hundred and fifty miles. Then this would be over.

4

HUMAN MOUTHS

"You know what I missed most?"

"No," said Maureen. "I have no idea."

"What I missed were mouths! People's mouths!"

"You didn't," said Maureen. The sun was still low but strong, mists rising with perfect focus into the sharp air. Trees were penciled in silver and light flashed between the branches in spokes. Ahead, traffic carried diamond sparks while the land stretched out, glittering and frozen-white. Maureen flapped down the visor. All that sunlight was giving her a headache.

"Months and months of masks! You know, I just hated not seeing what people's mouths were doing!"

"I know what you mean," said a second voice. This one sounded older than the first and more solid. Maureen pictured a woman with gray hair and one of those linen shift dresses that hid things, whereas the voice of the first suggested some-one who was altogether slimmer and more golden. She spoke in exclamation marks.

She was doing it again now. "People say you read a person's face from the eyes! But that's not true!"

"You're right," said Gray-hair. "I've never thought that way before, but now you say it, I know exactly what you mean."

"It's the mouth that tells you what a person is feeling!"

"Oh, you're so right."

"You know what I find? I just want to hug people! I see them going about their lives and I just want to hug them! Complete strangers!"

"Well, that's it," said Gray-hair. "If there's one thing we learned from the pandemic it was that people are kind. The kindness of strangers. It's what kept us going—"

Maureen reached for the radio. "Oh, what utter tripe," she said. And she turned it off.

Maureen was not an easy person. She knew this. She was not an easy person to like and she wasn't good at making friends. She had once joined a book club but she objected to the things they read, and gave up. There was always someone between her and everyone else and that was her son. This year he would have turned fifty.

After his suicide thirty years ago, her grief was so great she thought she would die of it. Really, she couldn't understand how she was not dead. She wanted time to stop. Paralyze itself. But it didn't. She had to get up every day and face his bedroom,

the chair where he sat in the kitchen, his great big overcoat
with no son inside it. Worse, she had to go out and face women
with children, and young men who were high or drunk, and
she had to walk past them without screaming. What had she
been supposed to do with that unbearable burden? The incredible anger that was eating her alive? There had been a few cards
of condolence—*We are sorry for your loss*; *Our deepest sympathy*—
a picture of a white lily, the embossed message in flowery gold
italics. Harold had found some comfort in those cards. He
even put them on the mantelpiece so that Maureen could find
comfort in them too. But she stared at the words and despised
them. Nothing about them made sense, in the same way that
going to sleep made no sense either. And the more she looked
at them, the more she felt accused—as if, without anyone saying it, they believed she must be to blame. In the end, she cut
the cards into a hundred jagged shreds, and when that did not
make her feel any better, she took the same scissors to her
lovely long brown hair and cut that off too. Oh, she felt mad.
Absolutely hopping. She didn't even recognize who she was.
She was just this new person, this raging sonless mother, the
shadowy figure you glimpse behind a pair of net curtains. The
future she'd meant to have was gone. She had no idea how she
was living this kind of ghost life instead, in which she could do
nothing except watch the person who had taken her place and
hate her. All she wanted was her son. All she wanted was to see
David.

"So if you think you want my husband, take him," she had
said to Queenie, when she paid a visit a few weeks after the
funeral. It was the first and only time they met, though Harold

used to tell stories about her at work—they seemed to share the same sense of humor—and Maureen could smell her in the car sometimes, a mix of violet sweets and cheap scent. Queenie had found Maureen hanging up the washing in the garden. She had come up the path holding out a bunch of flowers that Maureen put straight in the laundry basket. "But if you don't want him," she'd told her, "clear out of our lives." They'd stood, the two of them, either side of the washing line while Maureen continued to peg out clean T-shirts that her son would never wear, and Queenie wiped away tears. "Haven't you gone yet?" Maureen shouted.

In her grief, she had said the worst things. Queenie was Harold's friend. She would never have taken him. But Maureen no longer cared in those days whom she upset. She wanted to upset them. She wanted to drive them all as far away from her as possible, to the other end of the earth, if she could. Even Harold. "Call yourself a man?" she'd railed. "Call yourself a father? It was your fault! I don't even want to look at you!"

It was only after Harold's walk that Maureen had finally been able to apologize. "Forgive me," she had said, and he had taken her hand and clutched it for a while as if he had never held anything quite so precious and said, "Oh, Maw, you were never to blame. Forgive me, too." She thought they might dare to have conversations about David and all the things they had got wrong. All the lurking, shadowy things she wanted to say and for which she could not find the words. But Harold was so exhausted in the weeks and months after his journey that those conversations never even started. She got the impression he had found some kind of release, an absolution of a kind, while she—who had gone nowhere—was left high and dry. She took up gardening again, though, because he had once loved to see her in the garden, almost as much as he'd loved her long brown hair. She redecorated the sitting room with patterned wallpaper and had the lino on the kitchen floor replaced. She chose a new color for the bedroom and made curtains to match the counterpane. She even cleared David's room, wrapping his things up, one by one, and placing them in a box for the loft. But she still kept a space for her son inside her. It was where he came from, after all. That small creel inside her.

Weston-super-Mare. Clevedon. The early morning was a tender blue, fading to milk on the horizon, and the frozen land rose and sloped away with white glowing spills. Gulls reeled, yawing and screeching, so many they were a broken crisscrossing of lines, while above them vapor trails tacked a path across the sky. Bundles of mistletoe hung in a line of trees, like oversized handbags. Approaching Bristol, she reached the stretch of motorway that was raised on columns, carrying it above woodland and the bowl of a valley. She passed over the River Avon, and saw light glinting on all the hundreds of cars parked at the compound of Portbury Dock, while far out there were the tall cranes and liners at the Severn Estuary. Maureen stopped at another service station, but only for water and the washroom. It wasn't as clean as it should have been and she had to put paper on the toilet seat. She washed her hands carefully.

A woman in a coat with big flowers all over it was crying and saying, "I don't know why I bother. I don't know why I keep going back," and her friend was holding her and saying,

"The trouble is you're a saint. You're your own worst enemy," while she pulled paper towels out of a dispenser and passed them to her friend. Maureen made a deal of stepping round them because they were also in the way of the hand-dryer.

"Your mother is a saint." It was something her father had often said. "She is a saint for putting up with me." And Maureen would wish he wouldn't because it made him sound so old and given-up.

The service station was busy. There were families everywhere, with children running all over the place. Twice she had to stop in her tracks. A man in a T-shirt with the words *Dining Area Host* was picking up trays of leftovers, one at a time, and trudging with them toward a screened-off section in the middle. Maureen didn't know when that term had come about. She didn't know why it was a better word than "cleaner." She passed a Lucky Coin game arcade and a Krispy Kreme doughnut display beside a row of those large gray plastic armchairs that gave a massage if you put money in the slot. An old man was asleep with his feet curled up and his face mask over his eyes. Maureen had hated the first time she wore a mask but that was only because it was like being squashed. She had grown used to it very quickly. And she liked the anonymity. The polite keeping of one's distance. After all, she'd never been what you would call a hugger. She didn't even like people calling her by her first name—that was another thing she'd disliked about the book group, apart from the trash they chose to read. It was all Deborah this and Alice that. So if Maureen had to wear a mask for the rest of her life, she could think of worse things.

"Could I interest you in a book?" said a woman, arranging a table of secondhand paperbacks in aid of Help for Heroes.

"Not my thing," said Maureen. She didn't even stop to browse. You never knew what you might find. It was enough to bring a fluttering feeling to her chest.

In the shop, she went in search of a bottle of water. Blue feet-shaped arrows directed customers in single file, which Maureen followed, though the couple coming toward her in matching animal-print fleeces did not, so she had to step aside for them and they didn't even say thank you. "Well, thank *you*," she said, under her breath.

There were more notices about social distancing and hand sanitizer stations, with spots of gel on the floor. But there was still nothing to make her want to go round embracing complete strangers, or even understand humankind any better. She paid for her water and a crossword magazine and no one asked her where she was going or if she was making good time.

The cashier had beautiful long fingers with green nail varnish, and a name badge that said "Moonbeam."

"Can I interest you in the special offer?"

"That depends," Maureen said. "What is it?"

"Three air fresheners for your car for the price of two." Moonbeam pointed at a display of them.

"But I only have one car," said Maureen. The air fresheners confused her. They were a selection of neon-colored tropical fruits, like pineapples and melons, and all of them with sunglasses on.

"It's still a bargain. If you lose one of your fresheners, you'll have another two."

"But if I have three fresheners, it means I'm waiting to lose one. And if I'm waiting to lose one, I will."

"It's up to you. I'm just telling you the special offer. You don't have to buy it." Maureen had barely turned before the cashier looked at the four young women behind her in the queue and gave a rolling of the eyes.

Harold had met kindness on his journey. Or he had brought out love in other people. But it was not like that for Maureen. "A difficult child," she heard her mother saying. Now she thought of them, the words seemed so clear, and she could see her mother in her patent shoes with three straps, which she was always polishing because of the mud outside. She could remember the smell of her mother too, always the same, always redolent of everything most longed for and most elusive. Her mother had been beautiful once and had airs. She came from good stock, was what she liked to say, but her husband had poor health and little money and they had been forced to retreat to the countryside. Her mother hated everything about the countryside. The smells, the dirt, the isolation. It mortified her that they couldn't afford extra help. "You think a house cleans itself?" she would say, in her sliced accent, holding a mop as if her dislike for it was personal, and Maureen would watch her and vow, *I will never be that person.* She was her father's child.

Yet these days she experienced a faint shock when she met her reflection in the mirror. Despite her short white hair, Maureen had her mother's mouth and chin. Even her way of holding her head high. You think you will be different but the blueprint is still there: Maureen looked into the mirror and saw the ghost of her mother, staring back.

Mid-morning. Signs for Stroud, then Gloucester, Cheltenham. The Cotswold hills were a dust-blue shoulder to her right. She passed a broken-down HGV, its cab jackknifed forward like a broken neck. Already the day was losing its sharpness. Vast scarps of cloud lay ahead, while the air felt full and there were still dark borders of ice on the hard shoulder where the sun had not reached. Fog was coming. A coach swung in front of her, St. George flags at the windows and football fans waving. She overtook a convoy of trucks carrying ready-made prefab homes, each with a set of net curtains at the window, and a woman whose car was packed to the roof with bin bags. By the time she reached the M42, the fog was so thick she could see it flickering toward the windscreen, like grains of sugar. The only color now was the smudgy red of taillights ahead; wind-crippled trees at the roadside appeared to grow out of water. The world had become a strange emptiness of road and mud-banks, where things had no connection, dissolving then solidifying, and she thought that this was how it was with her mind. That it was a series of puzzle pieces that could never be put together.

WARNING. M42 CLOSED. Maureen was pulled back to the present. A sign flashed above the motorway, the orange letters spilling into fog. QUEUES AHEAD. She drove another few miles and tried to focus on the road but it was like driving into nothing and she kept losing concentration. She was far away again, thinking of David and his tablet at the crematorium that she visited every month and polished with a cloth, and the little green stones around it that she tidied with a hand-sized rake, even though other people did not tidy their little stones, so that they fell into David's and then she had to tidy those too. She was thinking of the large woman with loud makeup whom she had approached recently, because the stones on her plot were all over the place, and the urn was rusted over, and how Maureen had said it surely wasn't too much to ask her to look after it properly. The woman had told Maureen to mind her own bloody business, and in her panic, Maureen had replied that if the woman ate a better diet, she might not be so unhappy. She had actually said that. Those very words had come out of her mouth. One moment, they were safe in her head, offensive, yes, but somehow not seeming that way—because this woman was big, no question, she had many soft chins, all coated in that terrible makeup—and the next, there the words were, slap in the air, like great big posters. Too late, Maureen realized her mistake. The woman had come up close, so close Maureen could see the clogged orange pores of her skin and the creases in her purple eye shadow, and shouted that Maureen was a fucking insane bitch. So now, when she went to the crematorium, she wasn't able to think only of David, she was also thinking of that large woman with the makeup, and hoping she would not be there, and the whole place was tainted in her mind, in the same way the bookshop on the high street had become tainted a few years ago. Carry on like this, there wouldn't be anywhere left.

Maureen hummed to stop thinking. This was the problem with the car. Too much time trapped in her head. Better to be doing things with her hands. She hoped Harold was managing with the dishwasher. She hoped he could find the coffee and the cups. She should have left those Post-it notes in the kitchen, after all. She would come off at the next service station and phone home. Besides, she needed the washroom again. She had only to think about it and she needed it. In fact the more she thought about it, the worse it got. A kind of burning low down, a tight heat. She needed to stop thinking about it. She thought about Harold instead and the skin on his back that was still as smooth as ever, and how the first time she had seen him naked, she had been afraid even to touch him because she wanted him so much. She had never seen her parents so much as kiss. The road curved to the left and Maureen kept driving in a trance of red taillights, her mind with Harold, until it dawned on her that something was wrong and the thing that was wrong was that those lights ahead were not moving, while she was. She was moving toward them and they were stationary.

Maureen pressed the brake. Nothing happened. She cramped it harder but missed and got the footwell. The car kept traveling forward. She jammed her foot down but too fast because this time the car seemed to lose traction and instead of stopping made a swerve to the left, and then, despite everything she did, she was heading very slowly but at the wrong angle toward the hard shoulder, and for a matter of moments she could no longer remember how to stop a car, or even which pedal was which, she knew only that it was out of control, that she was sliding toward the barrier and there were other cars all around her, none of them moving, and beyond that, a wall of fog, and all her turning of the wheel and pumping of the brake made no difference.

There was a strange moment of stillness, an almost welcome realization that what she was trying to prevent was already happening and there was nothing she could do any more except sit very still and see what happened next. She badly needed the washroom.

5

SEA GARDEN

Queenie made a sea garden at her home in Embleton
Bay. Locals now call it the Garden of Relics because
of the things people leave there. But I only heard recently that she created a monument to your son. I
thought you might like to know that. Much love,
Kate x

To begin with, it had been a postcard that arrived in the
summer. Harold had read it out loud and they'd got on
with their morning. Maureen weeded the strawberries while
he sat in the sun. But her mind kept going back to it. "I didn't
know Queenie had a garden," she would say to Harold, trying
to keep the snag out of her voice, and he would smile and say
he didn't either. The fact was it was just a garden. A garden that

was four hundred and fifty miles away. If there was a monument to David, so what? Queenie had worked with Harold for all those years. They must have talked about David sometimes. But from there the garden grew in its awkwardness, like a splinter you don't attend to. Why had Queenie made a monument to David? What right had she to do that? And what was it like, this monument? Had Queenie known David? The questions came back to Maureen as she put out the washing or forked the vegetable beds. They returned to her in the lulls when she brushed her teeth or made Harold's breakfast or even as she lay beside him at night, wide awake while he slept. Time went by. The days shortened. The leaves changed. But her head didn't. She couldn't forget about the garden; it only became more insistent. It was out there and yet it was stuck inside her too.

"Are you sure you didn't know about Queenie's Garden?" she asked Harold, one evening over supper. "The one Kate wrote to you about?" It was autumn by this time. She tried to put the question in a casual way as if it was something that had just occurred to her.

"Queenie's Garden? I'm not sure. I don't think so."

"But she was a gardener, was she?"

"I don't remember that she was a gardener. We never spoke about gardening. At least, I don't think we did."

"Then why is David in her garden? Did Queenie know David? Why didn't I know she knew him?"

The impatience in her voice betrayed her. She was asking too much too quickly and now he was looking pained, as if he suspected he had done something terrible that he should remember without knowing what it was. "Oh dear," he said. "Oh dear." He touched his head with the heel of his hand and tapped it, trying to wake things up. "It will come back, it will come back, give me a moment." But it didn't. She picked up the dinner plates. Scraped his leftovers on top of hers. Took them to the sink and rinsed the plates with hot water.

"Can I help you, Maureen?"

"It's fine. You just sit there." She hadn't intended it to come out like that. The blow was cheap. He came up behind her. Snaked his arms around her waist and rested his chin on her shoulder. He was tired and she felt it, then. What she'd done to him, bringing all this back about David.

He said softly, "It was a long time ago, you see."

"I know it was."

"The garden is nothing to worry about."

"I know."

"We're happy."

"We are."

"So let's not worry."

"No, Harold. We won't."

He kissed her and the subject was closed. But even though she'd agreed not to, she did. She did worry. And the fact that he didn't want to made her double-worry—as if she had to take it on for both of them. It had been the same after Queenie died and the director of the hospice sent on Queenie's letter. Harold hadn't wanted to worry about that either. It was Maureen who had pored over the pages, trying to understand from the packed script that held no words, only dashes and squiggles, what Queenie had been so desperate to tell him. Trying to understand what he didn't wish to know. In the end she had tucked the letter into a shoebox and stowed it in the loft, along with David's things. But she was too old for this now. They were both too old. She didn't want it all welling up again. Only it had already begun. The ghosts had entered the room.

Alone, Maureen searched for images of the garden on the computer. She was shocked. There were all these people who had visited it, people she didn't know. Taking selfies and family portraits, or artistic wide shots. So they must have seen Queenie's monument to David. They had seen it, and Maureen had not. Where was it, then? What did it look like? Was it an exact image of him? Or something more contemporary? She looked and looked, and she tried to make the images larger, but she couldn't find him anywhere. She couldn't find anything that looked remotely like her son.

The truth was it wasn't just David she couldn't find. She couldn't make sense of the garden, full stop. It didn't even appear to have a fence. It simply came out of the dunes. There were stretches of shingle, interspersed with circles of stones and flowers and metal sculptures that were all kinds of shapes—funnels, tubes, spirals, spindles and whorls—alongside pieces of driftwood, some the size of wooden spoons but others as tall as posts, and dominated by one huge balk of timber at the center. There were strange sculptures too, made out of plastic bottles, guttering, tin cans, old furniture, rope and brushes—the kind of things, in fact, that she wouldn't think twice about throwing away. There were even poles with weather-bleached animal skulls on top. She looked at all this as if she was staring at life from the other side of a steamed-up window that she couldn't rub clean. Banners of seaweed and cork floats were strung between sticks, or hung like necklaces over single pieces. Ribbons were tied to branches. There were seed heads as bold as pieces of ironwork and grasses the size of sprouting fountains. In summer, all this was thrown into relief by the bright splashes of yellow and orange and red from gorse, marigolds and poppies. (You could tell it was summer because the sky was blue and the people visiting the garden wore sunglasses and T-shirts.) On other occasions, it appeared to be lit by hundreds of tiny candles. At the back stood an old painted wooden chalet with a falling-down roof.

Winter came. Harold and Maureen got on with life. They ate together and slept together but they were in separate circles all over again. He was happy watching for birds, and playing drafts with Rex, while she was cooped up by herself with the computer, searching for Queenie's Garden online and getting more and more agitated. Besides, as far as Maureen was concerned, a garden was a garden. It was for growing things to eat. Swede and onions and potatoes and spinach and fruits to freeze or bottle and take you through winter. It wasn't for bits of junk and wood and metal. So it wasn't simply that David was there, but more that he had been made a part of something from which Maureen was excluded. It was like looking at those cards of condolence all over again. And then she'd had a nightmare that disturbed her so much she'd had to go downstairs and turn on every single light in the house until day came and Harold woke.

"What happened, Maw sweetheart?" He put his arms around her and she rested her head on his shoulder as she began to tell him her dream.

It was about digging in a vegetable bed and finding David all alone beneath the earth, though she stopped short of talking about the worms that poured out of his mouth and ears, or the side of his face that was so decomposed it was a black layer of rotting leaves. She couldn't bear to say those things about their only son, even after all this time. Best to keep those dark thoughts to herself.

"I'm sorry. I'm not like you, Harold. I can't stop dwelling on Queenie's Garden." She described all the images she'd seen online that she couldn't make sense of.

It was then that he gave one of his smiles that still unbuttoned her slightly and told her he'd been wrong. She needed to go and see it.

"Oh, no," she said quickly. She got up. Straightened a few things. Wiped her hand on a chair, checking for dust that was not there. "No, no. There's no need to do that. No, no. It's much too far. Who would look after you? No, no. I'm just talking about it. That's all."

"You're right, of course. It's a very long way. But why don't you think about going? You could do it over a few days. Kate's a kind woman. She lives about twenty miles away. You could stay at least one night with her."

"Oh, no. No, I wouldn't want to do that. I wouldn't want to stay with Kate. I don't know Kate. She's your friend. Not mine."

There were so many reasons she couldn't go, she said. It wasn't just the distance. There was the house and the washing and everything else: she was even thinking of replacing the old pink bathroom suite with something more neutral. The truth was she was slightly scared of Kate, though she had never met her, just as she was scared of Queenie's Garden. Kate was in her late fifties, and some kind of activist. She had decided to give her marriage another try after walking with Harold but it hadn't worked and now she lived alone. That was all Maureen knew. Of the many people he had met, Kate was the one he cared for most, which was another reason Maureen felt insecure when she thought about her. Maureen wasn't sure she would even know what to say to an activist.

But she had got herself cornered. And, true to form, she'd achieved it all by herself. In the end she had to agree. Harold was right. Yes, she would go to see the garden, but she would get the drive over and done with in one day. Rex agreed to look after him while she was gone, though privately she suspected that, with Harold's forgetfulness and Rex's heart, it would be more like two small boys holding hands.

"I won't visit Kate. I'd rather keep this to myself. I'll order a shop for you and Rex online. And I'll show you how to use the dishwasher. It isn't difficult. It's just some buttons. I'll leave a Post-it note . . ."

This time he laughed. "Even we can work out how to wash a few pots and pans."

She wrote instructions anyway and found a nice guesthouse called Palm Trees near Embleton serving early-evening meals, and booked it for two nights. She would drive there on the first day, see the garden the following morning, and set off for home early the next. She made so many meals for Harold and Rex, there was barely room for them all in the freezer. If she kept herself busy, she felt more in control. The evening before, she packed a few necessary things, then pressed her best blue blouse to the thinness of a paper cut-out, while Harold found a wire brush and cleaned her driving shoes. Like preparing armor, she thought briefly, except no one was going to war. It was just a garden with some driftwood in it, and that was all.

He smiled at her and maybe he caught hold of what she was thinking, because he said, "It's okay. There's nothing to be frightened of."

"I know."

But she watched him later as he slept, his hand loosened from hers and now neat on his chest, his breath going pop, pop, pop, and she envied the peace it brought him. He is the brave one, she thought. The complete one. Not me.

6

ACCIDENT-ACCIDENT

By Tamworth, the fog was so thick she could barely see beyond a few yards. The watery outline of trees seeped into air, with crows roosting in the branches like big black buds. There was no horizon and no sky. You might have thought this was the only place left in the world, a service station on the M42. Maureen phoned Harold from the car park, once she'd had a change of clothes. The coach of football fans spilled out of the entrance, holding their flags above their heads and singing, "Eng-a-land! Eng-a-land!"

Harold said, "An accident? What do you mean, an accident? Are you hurt? What happened?"

"No. The car is fine. There's not even a dent on the bumper." The air wrapped itself around her, like a wet bandage.

"I wasn't worrying about the car. I'm not worried about the car at all."

"Well," she said, "that's because you don't drive any more."

He gave a soft and slightly creaky noise that she knew was him smiling. "No, Maureen. It isn't because of that. It's because you're my wife and the car isn't. The car is a car."

"Well, I just wanted to say I'm fine. Nothing broken." She was talking in an oddly bright voice she didn't like, but she couldn't bear to tell him about the other car that had stopped or the young man who had got out to help her. From the motorway she heard sirens and saw flashing blue lights within the fog as police and ambulances wove north. "Now they've closed the M42 completely. There's been an accident."

"Another accident?"

"Yes. Not like mine. Mine was nothing. I only hit a patch of black ice and swerved into the hard shoulder. This was a lorry. I have to follow a detour."

"Poor you."

"It could add another hour. More, maybe. I don't know." She held tight to her mobile. She didn't want him to hang up. Not yet. But she also didn't know what to tell him. Out of nowhere, she had a picture in her head of him tying back brambles once on an overgrown path, so that other people would not get hurt. It was such a Harold thing to do. She wanted to cry but she could not let herself. "How is Rex?" she said. "Is he with you?"

"Yes. Rex is here. We're playing drafts."

"Hello, Maureen!"

"Ask him if he took his pills."

"Maureen says, 'Did you take your pills?'"

"Yes, Maureen!"

"Have you been eating properly?"

"Very well."

"Don't just eat sandwiches."

"We won't."

There was a moment of silence that felt longer than it was. Harold said slowly, "Are you all right, Maureen?"

"Of course I am. I've had a bit of a shock, but I'm fine."

"You're sure?"

"I'm positive."

"So long as you're sure. You know I'm here whenever you need me."

"So am I, Maureen!"

"Thank you," she said. "Tell Rex thank you too."

"We know you can do this."

"You can do this, Maureen!"

"Make sure you drive carefully."

"I will. And don't forget to eat."

"We won't."

"Promise me. Not just sandwiches all day. Sandwiches are not enough. They're not a proper meal."

And he said yes. He promised. "Not just sandwiches," he said. "We will eat proper meals."

This was what she did not tell him. Could not, in fact. About the kindness of the young man who had stopped to help her.

The kindness that had made everything a hundred times worse. Because there she had been, with the front of her car at an angle and right against the barrier of the hard shoulder, shocked but not injured, and not a disgrace either, when a young man pulled up behind and leaped out. He signaled at her to unwind her window and leaned down to ask if she needed an ambulance. He was wearing no coat, in her distress she somehow noticed that, but he looked clean, his chin shaved soft and pink, his parting straight, and his sweater ironed—the sort of young man her mother had once hoped Maureen would marry. She insisted nothing was wrong but he wouldn't go away. He was hell-bent on being helpful. Suddenly all she could think about was a tight-bunched feeling in her bladder.

"You might be in shock," he was saying. "Is there anyone you would like me to ring? Are you sure you can move your legs?"

"I need a washroom," she said, in her best telephone voice.

"Come again?"

Too late. She had wet herself. Right there in front of the lovely clean young man with no coat. She moved her legs to keep him happy and it all just happened. An involuntary dissolving of her body that briefly felt delicious, followed by a terrible warm flow between her thighs. Afterward the traffic began to move again, but slowly, and she had to reverse into the waiting queue, with this man now in his car behind her, knowing full well what she had done, and she had to drive twenty miles in that slow procession of traffic, sitting in her own wetness. She was disgusting. She said it aloud, "You are disgusting, Maureen Fry." And then she had to walk into the service station with something from her suitcase, hiding her behind with her handbag. She headed straight for the washroom and there she yanked out a wedge of paper towels and soaked them with water before locking herself inside a cubicle.

"Pooh-ee. That old lady *stinks*," she heard a child say.

She could have died. She could have died of the shame. She waited for someone to use the hand-dryer before she stuffed her soaked underwear into one of those bags for sanitary towels and shoved it into the bin. Then she had dressed—all the while balanced in that tiny cubicle—in her clean underwear and slacks that were supposed to be for tomorrow, trying her best not to get them on the tiled floor because it too was wet, while everywhere she looked there were poster adverts for period-proof underwear. Oh, the world made no sense. She walked out of the washroom with her chin high, but feeling scorched. In the shop, she found antiseptic wipes and took them to the self-checkout because the last thing she wanted was any kind of conversation with another human being.

And now here she was, back at the car, cleaning the driver's seat. She should have listened to the assistant with green fingernails. She should have bought those three air fresheners.

"Okay," a man was saying to his wife, as they passed. "Okay. I may not know what I'm talking about but anyone with any sense would agree with me." They each nursed a tiny dog in the crook of their arms.

Maureen drove on. From Tamworth the traffic was directed to Atherstone, but then there were roadworks and yet another detour. A detour of a detour. She didn't know that was even possible. Worse, the smell was still on her and it was in the car too and all she could think of was a hot shower. She tried to keep her mind on the road ahead and not allow her thoughts to drift but it was hard when everything looked the same. "I want a dog! I want a dog!" David used to say. There was a Christmas they had given him a fluffy toy that went, "Woof! Woof!" when you pressed a button, and even sat on its back paws, as if it were begging, and he had said, "Oh! A dog!" But she had caught him afterward, staring at the garden with the toy dog back in its box, and she had known, with a dropping away in her heart, the disappointment.

The traffic reached a standstill on a dual carriageway. The banks were littered with plastic. Fly-tipping: a row of ten bin bags someone had arranged in a line. She was behind the coach of football supporters again. They waved their flags out of the windows and she watched anxiously, not wanting them to notice her. People began to get out of their cars and lorries and walked where pedestrians were not allowed to go. They climbed the central reservation and tried to see what was going on ahead. They got out their phones and even spoke to one another, complete strangers. Then the football fans jumped down from the coach, carrying beers and waving their flags, knocking on people's car windows. Maureen sat very tight and still. A car of young women waved to the football fans and got out too, laughing, even though they were dressed in tiny tops that were more like bras, and began sharing beers with them, as if they were in a club. Young people, thought Maureen. There was something about the glint in their eye, and the carelessness. And yet she had been the same once. Hard to believe, but she had thought she was on the cusp of the future. She had honestly believed history was all a kind of rehearsal and the real business of life would begin, with Maureen at the center. She would pass her school exams with flying colors and go to university to read French—no one else in her village had gone to university—and life would happen. She would meet other people like her, gifted and exalted, clever people, who wore berets and smoked those French cigarettes and talked about philosophy. Not that she had read any yet, but she would. Hadn't her father always told her? She could do anything if she put her mind her to it.

Ahead, the traffic began slowly to move. People got back in their cars. Beyond the fog, she saw nothing but industrial units the size of hangars.

On and on. So slow it would have been quicker to walk. Briefly the fog cleared and the sun threw out pale arms as if it were drowning in cloud. A gorse bush flashed yellow sparks. After another half-hour, Maureen pulled over at a lay-by to stretch her legs. There was one of those vans where you could buy burgers and kebabs and the smell was of overheated rubber and hot fat. She was too exhausted to eat but she finished her flask of coffee.

At the opposite side of the lay-by, a man was sitting alone in the back of his car, with the windows steamed up. He seemed not to be doing anything. She even wondered if he was asleep. Suddenly he opened the door, walked to the bin and emptied a plastic bag of water bottles and polystyrene food trays into it, then smoothed his plastic bag and folded it into a neat square. He pulled a toothbrush out of his pocket and a tube of toothpaste, cleaning his teeth and spitting onto the ground, before returning to his car and getting once again into the backseat.

He was wearing smart casual clothes. If he had seen her, he didn't acknowledge it.

As Maureen drove on, she thought about the man in the car and wondered how long he had been there. Days, probably. It was possible he had no home. But there was only so much you could see of another person's trouble without getting lost yourself. Better not to get involved in the first place. A truck slowly overtook her, piled high with discarded Christmas trees. A flock of crows flew out, like charred scraps.

In her mind, Maureen was back in David's room. After Harold's walk, she had decided to redecorate that too. She had chosen a bright shade of yellow and taken down the blue curtains and made flowered chintz ones instead. It had felt right. Like a fresh page. Peaceful, even. She put a desk in there, thinking she might try her hand at poetry, though the few times she tried, she gave up. The words she wanted would not come, or lost their color the moment she put them together. It was no wonder she'd flunked her exams at school and ended up at secretarial college instead of university: it turned out she was not so special after all.

David's room had stayed the same for several years, sherbet yellow and empty. She could go past his closed door without hurting, or even feeling the need to go inside and talk to him the way she once used to. It was the pandemic that changed things. Everyone forced to stay at home. She found herself going back into the room, if only to be in a different space. And it had struck her then with a force that made her weak how ferociously empty it was, and how ghastly and yellow, and how much she did not like those flowery chintz curtains. She did not like them one bit. So she had begun to fetch things of David's out of the loft and put them back. His books, his trinkets, his photographs. One by one. She even found his old blue curtains and re-hung them. Harold had said nothing. Maybe he didn't notice. Sometimes she thought they were heading in opposite directions—as if she was now responsible for carrying all those things he felt free to let go. And yet the room was all wrong. Even if she made it blue again, she would still see the yellow. She would still know she had tried to pack David's things away. It left her with a bitter, vinegary feeling. The only thing she had left of David was his room and, look, she had vandalized it.

From far away came a fresh memory of looking at him as a baby when he was so small and black-haired, and realizing, with a sense of responsibility that terrified her, that nothing lay between him and the loneliness of the world except her, all her love and her fear, but mostly her fear, because if anything happened to him, she would not be able to bear it. She would not survive. She had never known such silence as the moment she found out he was dead.

Maureen pictured the trinkets she had placed back in his room—a china zebra and a wooden horse and a glass deer, the photograph of him as a baby. Such meager scraps on which to heap all her great love. The emptiness stretched between them on the shelves. Where were all those words he had once told her that she must have forgotten, or misunderstood, all those stories, all those ideas, never realizing how little she would have left of him one day? How was she supposed to bear the weight of so many things she still couldn't understand?

The traffic poured back onto the M1. Loughborough, Keg-worth. Nottinghamshire at last. *Welcome to Robin Hood County!* Maureen shook her head. She groaned. All this relentless thinking and remembering, and she had still over two hundred miles to go. Stuck in the car, she was exposed only to herself, with no Harold to dilute her. Smoke tumbled upward from chimneys. The coach of football fans was back and they pointed down at her and laughed, and even though it surely wasn't pos-sible they knew what she'd done earlier, she couldn't help feel-ing that they did. She thought of home, where everything was clean and in the right place, and the pink bathroom suite with its brass taps and matching pink tiles, which didn't need re-placing, not really, and she thought of Harold padding down-stairs in his bare feet that still bore the scars from his walk to Queenie. She thought of the man living in his car and how much she did not want to dwell on other people's sadness.

Maureen swung off at the next exit, and pulled over at the first garage. She didn't even make it to a proper parking space. She reached for her mobile and as soon as he answered she told him she'd made up her mind. She was turning round.

"But why?" he said. "Why?"

"Harold, I had an *accident*-accident. It wasn't just the car. I wet myself. I actually did that. And now I'm wearing my clothes that are supposed to be for tomorrow and I want a shower, Harold. I want a shower. I can't do this. I'm not like you. And I've only just passed Nottingham. I won't even get to the guest-house in time for dinner. I'm coming home."

There was a pause during which he said nothing and then there came his voice with its familiar soft creakiness.

"Oh, Maw. We're getting older. That's all. But you wanted to see the garden. You couldn't get it out of your head. And now you're more than halfway. So why don't I look for Kate's number and ask if you can stay there for the night? It doesn't matter if you arrive late. You won't feel right unless you do this, Maureen."

Listening to him, she felt her heart swing wide open. He understood and accepted her for who she was, in the same way, many years ago, that she had watched him dance as a young man, all arms and jumping about, ignorant and out of place, and she had accepted him too. Maureen had not known what she was for until the day she met Harold: all she wanted after that was to stand between him and the rest of the world. In love and loved. It would be fanciful to say the fog was clearing but she thought there was a thinness to the cloud where she hadn't seen it before. A promise of blue, even if it wasn't there yet.

So Maureen did what he told her. She got back on the road. Rex texted her a list of directions to Kate's home and a smiley emoji.

Ten minutes later, her phone gave another ping from the passenger seat and there came one more text from Rex. This time it was an attachment to a map, with an arrow showing where she could stop at a service station and take a shower.

The emoji he chose was a unicorn with hearts for eyes. She didn't understand the point of it. But still. She smiled.

7

NORTH AND FURTHER NORTH

North, said the signs. Always north. Early afternoon and the fog was lifting. Chesterfield, Sheffield. Far away, the white-patched Peak District. Fields of wind turbines, like majestic blades on giant egg beaters, so strange close up they didn't look quite real. The land rose and fell, the earth giving way to houses and warehouses, slate-gray rooftops, and the outline of further cities and towns on the hinterland. Maureen drove below snatches of sky where sunlight glinted on the road, steel blue, spun gold, as rich as the glances off a crow's wing. Harold said there were as many different types of birdsong as countries in the world. He said it often, as if he had never said it before, always with wonder in his voice. Sometimes Rex recorded a bird call they didn't know on his phone, then went home to identify it on his computer. "Listen to this!" he would say later, rushing back and holding out his phone for her to listen. "What do you think it is, Maureen?"

"Sounds like another bird to me," she would say. "Who would like coffee?"

"Could I ask for two sugars, please, Maureen?"

"Oh, Rex," she would say, starting to laugh. "You honestly think I haven't learned after all these years how you like your coffee?"

At Tibshelf, Maureen had taken a shower. This was why she was happy. Who knew? Who knew there were showers in service stations? She had never so much as noticed one before—but there it was, a clean cubicle, behind a gray door with a picture of a showerhead on the front, and inside a set of hooks to hang her clothes. There was even a vending machine selling everything a human body might require, but in miniature form, including a doll-size bottle of body wash, a sachet of shampoo, a condom and a tampon. She had stood in that deluge of steaming hot water and it was almost as wonderful as the shower back at home.

The M18 and then at last the A1. Doncaster, Adwick le Street. Pontefract. Ferrybridge power station, with its disused cooling towers, like overturned pots. Maureen was entering North Yorkshire. An exit for Leeds. Wetherby. The sun sent down streamers of silver and gold light between clouds. A heron lifted into the air, as unlikely as a carpet bag taking flight. When she stopped at the service station, she was careful to be polite. She made a point of smiling at the young man mopping the floor in the washroom and telling him what a lovely clean place it was. When she bought a cup of tea, she thanked the barista a number of times, even though her hot drink was technically no more than a paper cup with some boiled water inside it, and a teabag in a separate sachet, and when the barista asked if she wanted anything else, she said, "No, thank you. That's perfect. Thank you." She found a table beside the window and asked the couple nearby if it was free, although it was very clearly empty and there was a plastic screen between them. She took out her puzzle magazine while she drank her tea and managed a whole cryptic crossword without being bothered by anyone. She even smiled at a table of four children who were all dressed as superheroes and eating KFC from buckets, while their mother swiped her phone and sipped a fizzy drink.

"I like your coat," she said to another woman, as she left.

"This old thing?" said the woman. But she tugged at the lapels and laughed.

"Yes, it's a lovely coat," said Maureen.

Back in the car, it struck her that really the coat was quite ordinary. It was Maureen's mood that was so likable. She switched on the radio, and when there was a song she knew, she hummed. A flock of geese flew overhead, their long necks straining north.

Already the day was over. That low January sky closing down. The spilled red of a winter sun. The land unfolded and cantilevered outwards, like breathing deeply. Ripon. Bedale. Scotch Corner. Durham. By the time she reached the Angel of the North it was dark again, the sky high-starred. The sculpture appeared before she expected it, leaning out of a hilltop ahead. It was hard to see, but the moon caught the span of its wings and she saw how wide out they stretched, how horizontal, not like ethereal wings at all, and she had the fleeting impression that if this angel came from anywhere, it would not be the heavens or the sky, but somewhere more human and earth-bound. Maureen made her way round Newcastle, crossing the Tyne, and finally turned off the A1 to head west. There were granite farms, scattered and isolated, their windows a buttery yellow. She passed beneath a tunnel of trees, and the light from the street lamps shone through the branches and made mosaic crystals on the way ahead. At last there was the sign for Hexham.

Maureen had been on the road for almost fourteen hours. She was so exhausted, and had seen so much, she felt bruised, marked all over, and the sound of the car engine seemed to have taken up residence inside her head.

She pulled up to check Rex's directions one more time, and applied a small amount of lipstick, then drove on to meet Kate. She could do this. She could.

8

TRUCK

When Maureen was a child, her mother dressed her in frocks and white socks. The frocks she made herself on her electric sewing machine and added details by hand like smocking to the bodice, or puff sleeves. The only time Maureen really remembered her mother laughing was when she ran her fingers over a new roll of organza. And Maureen had liked those frocks. She had believed her father when he said she looked like a princess, as if looking like a princess was a good thing when you're five and live in a farming hamlet slap bang in the middle of nowhere. It was only when she started school that it began to dawn on her she had been gravely misinformed. That a child in white lace, with a rosebud trim at the waist, or a moss-green silk sash with a bow the size of her head, is a walking target for other children, less fortunate, who will lie in wait for her as she skippetty-skips home in her little-girly frock, and they will splatter her with mud pies and worse. Similarly, that a child who carries a satchel and keeps her pencils sharp, and lays them on her desk in order of color, from dark to light, or who talks as if she has a plum in her mouth, or insists on telling the kind of long stories that so delighted her father, will never be popular. Will, in fact, become a laughingstock.

As Maureen approached Kate's, she experienced the same feeling she'd had all those years ago as a child, that same low-belly horror at having got everything wrong. Until that day, it had not occurred to her—because why would it?—that other children would not admire her superior clothes and her nice neat pencils and the way she believed she knew the answers to absolutely everything, even when she didn't, in the same way she had assumed Kate would live in a dear little cottage that she would have cleaned extra-specially since Maureen was coming to visit. In her mind, she had placed a casserole in the Aga that Kate would surely own—because even if she was an activist she still had to eat—and she had laid a table with a clean white cloth. In anticipation of these things, Maureen had stopped to buy wine and a box of chocolates.

Her mistake was obvious now she thought about the directions. No house name. Not even a number. Nor, come to think of it, a street name. Just instructions to follow a lane that turned out to be more of a wild track, and a few references to suspicious landmarks, like a disused phone box, and the old gates to a farm. Why had Kate never mentioned to Harold in any of her postcards that her home was no longer a home-home, in the traditional sense of the word, let alone a cottage, but actu-

ally a converted truck? And why had she omitted to say that it
was not on its own, this mobile home, but part of a community
of other campervans and trucks? All inhabited by the kind of
women Maureen read about in the paper, who lived in trees to
stop them being chopped down, or sat on bridges to protest
about global warming?

She had driven for what felt like miles down the track, eas-
ing the car in the dark around a pothole only to bump it into a
stone, and passed these trailers and caravans without giving
them so much as a second thought—until she reached a gate
that said "No trespassing." She'd had to reverse, because it was
too narrow to turn, hitting all the potholes and stones a second
time, but this time with more force because she couldn't see
them properly in the dark out of her rear windscreen and, anyway, reversing had never been her strong point. She stopped
close to the group of caravans and campervans, but she had no
signal to call Rex.

"Can I help?" A blue woman had knocked at her window,
with a rainbow shawl. The blue, Maureen later realized, was
because she was heavily tattooed. The rainbow was her hair.

Maureen wound down her window but not too far and said
she was looking for a person called Kate but she had made a
mistake.

"No. You're right. Kate is here," the young woman had said.
Her voice was as sweet as a child's. She could only have been in
her late twenties.

"Here?" said Maureen, unable to disguise her shock.

"That's right."

"I don't know where to park."

"Yeah. Here is cool."

"Here?" said Maureen again.

"Cool," said the young woman.

So Maureen straightened the car and parked, though she straightened it again, because with nothing to align it against, like a garage wall, it was hard to get it correct. Then she stepped out of the car, straight into mud in her driving shoes, and opened her boot, wondering if the rainbow-haired young woman might help with her suitcase, but apparently not because she had already drifted ahead.

Maureen followed her past the other caravans. Not wanting to dirty the wheels of her suitcase, she was forced to carry it. They passed about ten in all and she could see lights inside them and the silhouettes of other women. She hoped none of them would come out. She had no intention of meeting any more strangers.

"That's it," said the young woman.

"That's it?" Maureen repeated.

"Yeah. Mum lives there."

"Your mother?"

"That's right."

"Kate is your mother?"

So this was Kate's daughter. Kate had a daughter. Another thing no one had thought to mention to Maureen. And her hair might have been rainbow-colored but it would have benefited from a wash. Then Maureen remembered she was trying to be nice, so she said, "I do like your hair."

"Cool."

"I'll just go ahead, shall I?"

"Sure." Away she had drifted.

Maureen picked her way in her driving shoes past a group of empty plastic chairs, a firepit, stepped around a pile of wooden pallets, and squeezed past a child's purple bicycle. She thought of Harold cleaning her shoes only the night before and felt unbearably tired. Fossebridge Road seemed like another country.

The door opened before Maureen could knock on it. An unexpected blessing because until that point Maureen was not clear it was a door. From the truck came the cry, "Maureen!" A woman appeared, with wild gray hair woven with ribbons of fabric. She wore a thick green cardigan and large earrings that were feathers and beads, as well as many necklaces and something else that resembled a dream-catcher.

"Maureen, you poor love!" cried the woman, as she heaved down a steep set of steps and then threw her arms around her. "I'm Kate!" She kissed the side of Maureen's cheek. Completely uninvited. Maureen recoiled.

"It's such a joy to meet you. Come in, darlin', come in."

Maureen followed her up the wooden steps while Kate said over her shoulder how truly wonderful it was to meet her after all these years and how much she loved Harold. He had been such an inspiration, she said. She apologized that the truck was so cramped, and hoped Maureen wasn't surprised. Maureen made herself say no, no, it was a very nice place. "Very unusual," she said. She was aware of the artificial strain in her voice, and also the awful splodges of mud over her driving shoes.

Inside the truck, there was not one single place for the eye to rest that hadn't already been claimed by something else. It was like looking directly into a migraine. Tiny Buddha ornaments, chakra stones, hanging quartzes, crystals, candles, exhortations to find your inner goddess and your angels, shelves draped with purple curtains. Everything carried a thin layer of filth and was either broken or about to be. And the smell. Dear God. She'd thought she'd smelled bad. Incense sticks were puffing away in every corner. She could barely breathe. There was no Aga. There was no casserole.

Maureen produced the wine and chocolates from her bag and offered them to Kate, who said, "You shouldn't! You shouldn't!" and placed them on top of a unit covered with so many other things, Maureen was not certain her gifts would ever see the light of day. She felt a pang of remorse for them.

The place was a hovel. She could try as hard as she liked to be nice but there was no nice way of saying it. There had been the holiday chalet they'd stayed in every year in Eastbourne when David was a boy and toward the end, it was true, the place had seen better days. A smell of mildew when you opened the front door, and dirt-colored carpet to hide stains. There had been the roadside motel where she'd stopped with Harold on the way home after his walk, which she hadn't realized until too late was in the middle of a red-light district. But they could have been anywhere; he had slept and slept. It was Maureen who had eaten alone in the motel bar with a number of women who did not seem to be there for the pleasure of dining. But this. It had never occurred to Maureen that a person who sent postcards to Harold could live like this. It wasn't even clean. It especially wasn't clean.

The truck was designed like an open-plan studio—an idea

that had never appealed to Maureen—with a miniature kitchenette near the door, the cupboards made of hardboard, with a
tiny sink in the middle, and on the other side, a single ward-
robe space, hung with another purple drape, alongside a shower
that was a plastic-curtained cubicle, so narrow you would only
be able to stand in it sideways. Then there was yet another
purple drape, beyond which there appeared to be the world's
most uncomfortable sofa—more of a ledge—and a Formica
table with two chairs and a stool. An incongruously large wing-
back chair was covered with an old eiderdown that Maureen
would honestly fear to disturb. "What a lovely place," said
Maureen again. "Isn't this charming?"

She took off her coat, but there was nowhere to hang it so
she put it back on again.

"How long are you holidaying here?" she said. Her voice was
on its brightest setting.

Kate bustled through to the other end of the truck. She
seemed to be saying to Maureen that this was her home, not a
holiday let, and that it was also home to her daughter and the
other women living there. They had decided to exist as a community, sharing whatever they owned. It was the best decision
she had ever made, she said, apart from walking with Harold,
of course. At the front of the truck, Maureen could see now
there were two seats and a steering wheel.

Maureen was still holding her suitcase. Kate was only a step
or two away from the man in his car. She could not understand
why anyone would choose to leave their home to live in a ve-
hicle, and her confusion made her panicky. She and Harold
had been in the same house for more than fifty years. The idea

of not living at 13 Fossebridge Road, with all her things safe in the correct places, appalled her. Kate switched on the kettle and reached for two chipped mugs.

"So how are you really?" she said, as if there were two versions of Maureen, one behind the other, and she didn't believe the one who was standing at the front.

"I'm fine," said Maureen.

"Harold told me you've done the whole drive in one day. I can't believe you've done that. You must be exhausted. He said you're going to visit Queenie's Garden. I guess that's tough, huh?"

"It isn't really," said Maureen.

"Darlin'. You must be hungry."

Maureen was. She was starving. Her limbs were almost hot and shaking with it. She hadn't eaten since her sandwiches. But her mouth said she wasn't. "I'm fine, thank you. I don't even need a cup of tea. I'll just go to bed. Maybe you could show me to my room? It's been a long day."

Even as she said this, she experienced doubt and felt foolish, as if once again she was missing the point. There was clearly no other room, beyond the one they were standing in. Also, there was no bed.

"I thought you could have mine tonight," said Kate. She pointed out the thing that was a ledge, not a bed, and explained it folded out. She spoke again about how great it was to get to know Maureen at last, and how meeting Harold had changed her life, while all the time Maureen stared at the ledge and thought of her bed at home with lovely pressed sheets and Harold inside it. Kate was still talking. She was telling Maureen about her marriage now and how it was lockdown that finished it, though things were good with her ex, and he still lived in their old house.

"I don't understand," Maureen said. "You gave him your house?"

"Yes, Maw. I wanted a clean start."

The truck did not strike Maureen as a clean start. She tried to smile.

"And I wanted to be with my daughter and my granddaughter, you know?"

No, Maureen did not know, not until Kate pointed outside to the young woman Maureen had met earlier, caught in the light from the other trucks and caravans. Maureen could see she was holding a scrap of a child with long black hair. The little girl had her legs tucked around her mother and her head on her shoulder. Maureen experienced a coldness, a drawing-in. So Kate was a grandmother.

"Maple," said Kate.

"I'm sorry?"

"She is the light of my life."

"But her name is Maple? As in the syrup?"

Kate gave a polite not-quite smile, as if she wasn't sure whether Maureen was being deliberately offensive. "No, not the syrup. More like the leaf."

Oh, Maureen was exhausted. She was inside-out with it. All that driving and then all the people. People who had green fingernails and people who lived in cars and trucks and people who named their children after parts of nature. Harold had told her strange stories about his journey but he'd never mentioned anything like this. Her head was hurting. "You should come and visit us some time," she said. "Harold would love to see you." She imagined Kate's truck parked outside 13 Fosse-bridge Road and knew she didn't mean it.

"Yes, I will," said Kate.

She knew Kate didn't mean that either.

Nevertheless Kate showed Maureen how to unfold the ledge into what was basically a larger ledge and passed her sheets that were not ironed, but smelled clean enough. She said goodnight, though this time, thankfully, she did not attempt to hug her. Alone, Maureen unpacked her nightdress and put it on and cleaned her teeth. She got out her puzzle magazine but dropped it onto the floor and she was so tired she couldn't be bothered to bend and pick it up. She lay on the bed.

Bed was a kindness. There was nothing bedlike about the pull-outy thing with its lumpy mattress on which Maureen was now doing her best to relax. She was beyond tired. She lay rigid and uncomfortable but she must have fallen asleep with-out noticing because she was woken by voices outside the truck, and heard a faraway clock strike ten.

"You okay, Kate?" It was Kate's daughter, the sweet-voiced woman covered with tattoos. Maureen opened her eyes wide in order to hear more clearly.

"Yeah, sure," said Kate.

"Where will you sleep?"

"I'll hunker down with someone. It's no problem."

"So what's the story? With Maureen?"

"Well, it's been hard for her." At this point her voice dropped and Maureen couldn't make out any more words. Then she heard doors closing and the voices of other women calling to one another and laughing, asking how they were, if they needed anything.

"Good night, hon! Good night!"

It was quiet again but Maureen was too ill at ease to sleep. She had that feeling that she'd had as a child of being completely wrongly dressed, and with her things all precious and silly, but unable to change because her world presented no alternative. She thought of the kindness with which the women at the camp called to one another, the easy intimacy, and Kate, who had willingly given up her own bed, even if it was a ledge, and how she would never be like that. She got up and opened her handbag for a tissue and found the piece of paper on which she had written Lenny's instructions. Another invitation to connect that she had failed.

Maureen sat stiff in the wing-back chair, taking care not to trouble the eiderdown. She had no idea what to do with herself. If only she was back in her own kitchen, where everything was clean and stowed away, even the cups, their handles all pointing in the same direction. In her mind, she allowed herself to creep along the beige carpet of the hallway, passing the hooks where she and Harold put their coats, to the sitting room with its patterned wallpaper, its matching upholstered chairs, and the mantelpiece where she now kept a framed wedding photograph and a portrait of David, along with a china shepherdess that had belonged to her mother. And from there she began to think of the house in which she'd grown up that was always cold, and suddenly she could see her mother, industrious at her sewing machine, while her father apologized so much for being a burden that he became one.

If only she had been more like the other children. If only she had learned how to dress like them and talk like them, instead of being kept apart. She remembered now walking across the fields with her father, even though the farmer let his dogs run loose. How the dogs had come at them and barked at her father, who held out his hands to placate them and told her not to run but to be calm, and how she had refused to listen as the dogs came close and decided to run after all, so that one had jumped up then and, when her father put himself in front of her, had taken a bite at her chin and mauled her father's hand. Her mother had railed and railed at him and he had sat, so full of remorse he couldn't even look at Maureen. Her mother had called him weak and good for nothing, and he had shaken his head, bearing it all, and Maureen had wished that for once he would stand up for himself. And yet, after he died, her mother had lost all interest in life. She was dead within three months. It struck Maureen that a person could be trapped in a version of themselves that was from another time, and completely miss the happiness that was staring them in the face.

For a few hours, Maureen managed to doze. She woke with her body stiff, but at least it was morning. She dressed in her slacks and a fresh blouse, straightening the sleeves of her cardigan, then put on her coat and driving shoes and picked up her suitcase. She would have taken her wine and her chocolates if only she could find them.

Outside the first shade of pale was coming but it wasn't so

much light as a little less dark. There was an atmosphere of stillness across the camp. Each of the trucks and mobile homes was closed up and unlit, except one where Maureen heard a woman's voice softly chanting. Briefly she felt an intense longing for everything to stop so that she could go back and give it one more try. But how could she do that? It wasn't in her. It was not how she was made. Nothing for it but to do what she had learned as a child and hold her head high and walk away. In the distance, traffic gave a muffled glow along the horizon, moving north. Maureen clicked the fob on her car key and the car popped alight. Its enthusiasm struck her as frivolous. But she got in.

Maureen went without leaving a note. She went without saying thank you or goodbye. It wasn't as if she would ever see Kate again, or her awful truck. So she just left.

9

GARDEN OF RELICS

The morning sky was torn and tattered by the wind, and golden light shone through, flashing, then vanishing, yet she saw everything, the land and the light and the cloud—even wink snatches of the sea ahead—through another kind of fog, because the only thing she could think of was David. Thirty years. Thirty years of waiting and searching. And now she was finally going to see him. He was her one thought.

Maureen had driven straight from Kate's to Embleton. She'd rung Harold to check he was awake but she said nothing about what had happened. She didn't even mention the truck. She took care to talk only about the driving and the weather, and when he asked her what she had made of Kate, she told him that she had gone to bed as soon as she arrived. There hadn't been any time to get to know her.

"Oh, what a shame," he'd said, and she could hear the regret in his voice. "I always liked Kate."

"I'd better get going now," she'd said.

At Embleton, Maureen located the Palm Trees guesthouse, and stopped to check in. The receptionist was a friendly young woman sitting in a little booth with a toy plastic palm tree on the desk. She said Maureen's room was ready for her if she wanted, but Maureen explained she was just dropping off her suitcase before she went to visit a garden. "Queenie's Garden? The Garden of Relics?" said the girl, with her singing Northumberland accent. "Just past the golf club! You can't miss it! When my mother died, we scattered her ashes there! It's a lovely walk!"

The walk could be as lovely as it liked but Maureen had no intention of doing it. She took the car to the golf club and when the road became a dead end, she parked as close as she could and made the very last stretch on foot, never looking back, not once, but always forward. She tied on a headscarf but the wind still flapped her slacks and got at her ankles. Beyond the dunes lay a horizontal blade of sea, and a vast expanse of sky.

She followed a track that crossed alongside the golf course toward the shore: a number of wooden chalets stood on the dunes ahead, looking tiny beside the sea, and it was toward these that she made her way. At the end of the golf course, the path swung to the left with a hand-painted plywood sign for Queenie's Garden, shortly followed by another sign pointing the way over a small bridge. The signs irritated Maureen. She knew the purpose of them was to be helpful, but she felt she should instinctively know where to go without the help of ply-wood, and the fact that she didn't—the fact that she actually needed these signs—made them all the more irksome.

Once she got to the sand, she had to take care in her driving shoes because it gave way abruptly to soft, sludgy patches that might wet her feet. The tide was a long way out. Gangs of gulls and oystercatchers scattered through the sky, and the wind threw up balls of foam from the sea that skittered and tumbled across the land and finally broke into nothing. In the distance to her left, Dunstanburgh Castle was a jagged ruin on the ho-rizon, shaped like the tricky piece of a jigsaw puzzle. And all the time she was thinking, David, David, David, where are you?

The signs pointed along the foot of the dunes, offering a welcome, each one decorated with seaweed banners and plastic flowers and shell necklaces. *Bienvenue! Willkommen! ¡Bien-venido! Välkommen! Hoş geldin! Witaj!* She didn't see why they needed all those foreign languages. It was just showing off.

From the beach, the signs directed Maureen up a flight of wooden steps set into the edge of the dunes, leading to a clus-ter of chalets. The steps were so steep they were more of a lad-der, and scattered with sand; even though there was a blue rope to hold onto, it wasn't enough and she had to reach out to the thick grass for support. There were already tributes. A plastic wreath decorated with bright red baubles. A bunch of fake lil-ies. The wind was getting stronger and made a gushing sound all round her. Maureen approached the first of the chalets, a wooden house with rickety steps and a veranda, its door and windows boarded up with shutters and a padlock. The next chalet was painted green, with matching curtains at the windows, while another was more like a bungalow with slate roof tiles. The signs to Queenie's Garden kept pointing ahead. She could make out the outline of some of the shapes she had seen on her computer, like totem poles, and she slowed. Suddenly she had no idea what she was going to do. All this time she had been thinking about seeing David and never once had it dawned on her to question what that actually meant. What would happen when she was finally standing in front of Queenie's Garden.

Nothing Maureen had seen online had prepared her for seeing it in real life. Nothing she'd imagined either. The garden was even more of a mystery now that she was here. She had no idea where to look for David.

Beneath her feet there was rough grass, but ahead the ground became intricate patterns of shingle, flint and stones of different colors, set in squares and circles, and interplanted with skeletons of plants that had died back over winter, as well as gorse bushes shaped like candle flames. Between these stood pieces of driftwood, dominated by one tall piece at the center, while other monuments surrounding it were no bigger than spoons. They were made of all kinds of things. Spiraled pieces of iron, twisted links, rusted chains, with chimes of keys and holey stones, and scraps of plastic and wood. There were also banners that flapped between poles, and many, many glass jars containing candles. But the thing that astounded her most was the number of people.

Two men stood at the back of the garden, pointing out its various features, and nodding as if they agreed it was beautiful. A young couple were hand in hand, speechlessly absorbed in a pyramid of stones. Another woman sat on her coat with a notebook and pencil, sketching what she saw, while a man in a biker's jacket was fixing a padlock to a chain. Maureen could see now that there was a kind of path through the garden that she had not noticed before, leading to the painted hut at the back. It was like looking at something you have never seen, such as the bottom of the ocean, where nature is a vast and infinitely more exotic version of what you imagined, and you feel very small for having given it such a poor expectation.

There was movement from a corner of the garden, and Maureen realized with a jolt that another woman was very close by, bent over, wearing a hat with two pompoms, one on each side of her head. She was probably in her early sixties and she seemed to be digging at the stones with a trowel.

Maureen stayed on the periphery, unwilling to go any further but not yet able to leave, hoping the garden would make sense to her if she just kept staring, while other people continued to enjoy it. At last the woman put down her trowel. "Can I help?" she called.

"No, thank you," said Maureen.

So the woman stayed where she was and Maureen stayed where she was. She tried looking for David among the sculptures but she still had no idea what she was searching for—there was nothing that looked like David here—and just when she really needed them, there were no signs either. Besides, with all those other visitors in the garden, Maureen felt awkward and self-conscious. She tried walking a few feet to the left but it still made no sense to her so she went back to where she'd been before. The woman in the hat with two pompoms put down her trowel again and stood. "Excuse me? Are you lost?" she called.

"No. I'm fine."

"Is there something you're trying to find?"

"It's okay. I can manage."

The woman looked at Maureen a moment. Her hat seemed to accentuate the wrinkles in her face, like slashes in her cheeks. "Why don't you come in?" she said. "Take a proper look round?"

A strange thing to say since there was no fence to separate what was inside from what was out. And yet instinctively Maureen understood what the woman meant. That there was a hallowed space, which was the garden, while everywhere else was not—everywhere else was ordinary dunes and marram grass. Maureen stayed pinned in the same spot, her hands tight-knit, until the woman came right up close, then took a step to one side, making a gesture with her hand as if inviting Maureen through an unseen gate.

"This way," she said. She turned and made her passage through the garden.

Maureen dipped her head as she followed. Yet another thing she did not understand. Like crossing yourself when you enter a church, except that she was not a churchgoer. She did not even know where the woman was taking her.

The path was not a straight one, but went in curves around the boulders and pieces of driftwood and stone circles. Things flicked in the wind, like tiny pieces of washing, but as she passed, she saw they were photographs of many different faces and that there were written messages too and other strange mementos, like shoes and crosses, and keys and padlocks tucked between the stones. Candles were everywhere, as well as further sculptures made of bottle tops and pieces of colored plastic and foam. A gust of wind took up from the sea so that the ribbons and pieces of seaweed flew out and there was a clinking sound of bells and many chimes.

Maureen went slowly, as if she did not trust the stones beneath her feet—as if they might give way without warning. All she could think of was the day Queenie had come to visit with her flowers and waited while Maureen hung out her dead son's washing. The other people in the garden looked up as she passed and some smiled. Once again, she experienced that old feeling of being the wrong shape for the situation in which she found herself. Of being an intruder. She wished that—all those years ago—she had been kinder to Queenie.

The woman said, "I'm Karen. I'm a volunteer. I work here twice a week. It's your first time, isn't it?"

"Yes."

"I thought as much. I remember my first time. I cried and cried. It has that effect."

Karen smiled sympathetically at Maureen as if she were expecting her to weep, and Maureen turned away. The sun had broken through the cloud again and flared over the garden, catching the pieces of driftwood so that they appeared especially bright, their sides gold and purple. The chimes flashed silver.

"Are you a gardener?"

Maureen said she was, but just vegetables.

"Queenie grew vegetables too. She especially liked ornamental gourds."

"Oh, I never tried those. I'm more—ordinary. Beans and, you know, potatoes and things." She tightened the knot of her scarf.

"Most people come to visit in the summer, when the weather's good. But Queenie loved it best in the winter. I feel the same. Of course, when you work in a garden all year, you get to know it like a person. Every part has a story. Did you meet her?"

"No." She said it quickly.

"She was a very special woman. She left the garden to the people of Embleton Bay. At first no one was sure what to do with it. But it's become a tourist attraction. Visitors come from all over the world. Even China."

Maureen had no idea people might come that far. And no one would describe her as special, apart from her father when she was a child, and look where that had got her. She tried to smile but it didn't happen.

"Then people began leaving things of their own here. Padlocks at first. We had so many padlocks. After that they brought more personal things, like photographs and poems in bottles and even their own sculptures. We took them all away. But we began to think that Queenie would have wanted those things to stay. She was a curator, after all."

They passed several boulders that had been carved with names and a bright blue bird made of fragments of glass. Karen said, "Someone told me once that the garden was about love.

Since then, I've heard a few people say that. They even say it makes a noise of its own but people will believe all sorts of things. It's just the wind." Her voice was quiet, as if she was talking to herself. "Now this little shoe?"

She pointed at a child's shoe, so small it must have been a first one. It was weather-beaten to the point where the leather had lost its color and it was woven with ivy into a larger drift-wood cross. There were shells too, all threaded with the ivy. "I am glad someone felt they could leave that here."

Karen showed Maureen another sculpture, a heart shape, made of barbed wire. "I wonder what went on there," she said.

After that she moved to a line of photographs and touched each face with her finger, marking its presence. There were to-tems made of driftwood and old garden tools and one with a model of a dog and another with a bird skull. She talked about the people who had brought memorials to the garden, like a man whose husband had died in a car accident and a farmer who had lost her home because of mad-cow disease back in the eighties. People from all walks of life, she said. "I love to hear their stories."

"You mean they leave things?" Maureen still did not really get why the garden was considered beautiful. But even more she did not understand why people would feel free to leave pieces of themselves there. Things that were so deeply personal and private and could not be replaced.

Karen said there were still the original tributes in the garden that had been Queenie's. She had found a place for her mother and father—she pointed at a monument that was made of a spade, and another that was a sturdy branch—and also a curtain of feathers. "These were some female artists she once lived with. But they're flighty things. They're always blowing away." She laughed. "We have to keep finding new ones."

They were in the center of the garden now, standing beside the tallest driftwood piece. Karen glanced up at it and said, "There was a man Queenie cared about, I believe. Yes. I think this might be him."

Maureen was no longer hearing the words. She felt the shock in her own face. A kind of dropping away behind her eyes and mouth.

She looked at where the woman was pointing. It was a huge balk of timber. Ten feet or more. It was so strong it might have once been part of an old ship. Nevertheless she also knew that what Karen was saying to her was the truth. If Harold was anything, he was that piece of wood. Steadfast and solid. She would have liked to touch the surface, all those wrinkles and twists. To rest against the tall bulk of him and feel his goodness.

"But the only piece she ever gave a name to is the one she called David."

Maureen was not ready. Her thoughts had slipped over to Harold; the words came to her as a blow, like being hit when you're not even looking. To hear David's name from the mouth of a woman she did not know was as shocking as visiting his body at the funeral parlor.

"David?" she said.

"He died young. He took his own life, I think."

Maureen did not know what to say. She did not know how to arrange her face. She didn't even know where to look.

"Which one is that, then?" she said. "Which one is David?"

"Well." Karen smiled. "For a long time I got it wrong. I thought he was the figure over there." She pointed to a piece of driftwood that was set apart from the others, with a hole worn right through it. It must have been about four feet tall, but so slim it was hard to see how it had not split because of the hole: you could see through it to the other side. "That's not the saddest thing I've ever seen," Karen said quietly. "But it is one of them."

"But it's not David?"

"No. I don't think that's anyone. It's just a piece of driftwood Queenie took pity on. David is the one over there." She pointed to another figure, fastened in the shingle. "You see?"

Maureen was nothing but nerve endings. Oh, it was the most appalling thing. Crueler even than the rings of bruises around his neck that the undertaker had tried to cover with makeup. There were no words. There were no words for the horror she felt on looking at that terrible piece of driftwood. She felt dizzy. Mauled. The monument was a knotty V-shape, in height only about two feet, the wood weathered to dark gray, crooked and complicated, like a broken lyre, and worn away into sharp points at both ends. It was not a tragic structure, like the holed piece Karen had already shown her. This was angry; it was violent; it was separate and undeniable. Maureen thought of his bedroom that she had wrongly painted yellow. She thought of the tablet at the crematorium and the little green stones she was always tidying, and how he was not in either place, no matter how much she tried to find him. But this was David. This was him. Too fragile for the world and yet full of youth and complication and pomp and arrogance. She did not know how such a piece of wood could have survived the wind and rain and yet, secure in Queenie's Garden, it had held fast. All those years she had been calling for David, all those years of waiting, and he'd been here all along. Queenie had taken him.

"Would you like to see more?" said Karen. "Or have you found what you were looking for?"

Maureen's heart seemed to shrink inside her chest, trying to defend itself. It was the same sensation she'd had as a child, and during Harold's walk, and again in Kate's truck, of being measured against something she didn't understand and would never get right.

"Are you sure you're okay?" said Karen.

Maureen couldn't speak. She nodded.

"Can I get you something? A glass of water?"

She managed one "No." She managed one "Thank you."

But she was almost not able to walk in a straight line as she hurried along the dunes and down the steps to the beach. And all the while she could feel Karen's eyes on her, so that Maureen had the strangest feeling of watching herself from a distance, as if she had become a person alone and apart, even from herself.

10

A BAD NIGHT

That evening, Maureen ordered a light early supper in the Palm Trees guesthouse. After seeing Queenie's Garden she had walked toward Dunstanburgh Castle because she wanted to keep moving, but nothing pleased her. Nothing took her from her own thoughts. She hadn't even felt able to manage a crossword puzzle. The dining room was brightly lit with a bewildering number of plastic palm trees in all shapes and sizes. At another table, a well-dressed couple were talking to their son about working harder for his finals. Even though Maureen tried to get on with her own meal and not listen, she might as well have been sitting right with them. Their son kept pushing his hands through his shaggy hair and saying it was cool and not to worry, while the woman said, in her voice that cut through the room, "I don't understand. How is it cool, if you fail your finals? Tell him, Peter. If you don't put in the effort, you'll never get anywhere." Maureen thought, Dear God, how much longer must I endure this kind of thing? She folded her napkin and left her meal barely touched because her mouth had given up trying to eat.

Her room was nothing like the one on the website. It was narrow and drafty, with a loud carpet that must have been laid in the fifties. She took a shower and afterward she found an extra red blanket wrapped in polythene and put her clothes back on with the red blanket on top. She looked like someone rescued from an accident. She had no idea how she would sleep. The minibar was empty.

Maureen rang Harold and told him she was going to have an early night so that she could leave Embleton first thing.

He said, "So? Did you see Queenie's Garden?"

"I did," she said.

"How was it?"

"Well, it was, you know . . . It was fine."

"What about . . . ?" He couldn't do it. He couldn't say his name. She had to do it for him.

"No," she said. "I didn't see David. Kate was wrong. He isn't there."

"Oh." She could hear the sadness in his voice. The disappointment yet again. She should never have gone on and on about the garden. She should have let it be. He would have happily forgotten, if it hadn't been for her. "Oh, well," he said.

"To be honest, I don't really know why I came."

"You wanted to see Queenie's Garden."

"Well, yes," she said. "But I don't know why I thought that was a good idea. I don't know what I thought would happen."

"So what is it like?"

Maureen thought of the tall driftwood sculpture, and the V-shaped one close by. She thought of how she had wanted to touch the tall one, and feel the solid strength of it; surely it had once been the same for Queenie. She remembered the final letter Queenie had written to Harold that was all dots and squiggles, the pen nib pushed so hard sometimes it had stabbed right through the pages. To think Maureen had stored that letter in a shoebox. To think she had kept it safe when what she should have done was tear it up. Oh, she should have gone at it with the scissors. She had been right that day by the washing line: Queenie had wanted to take Harold from her all along. Maureen felt that old stinging bitterness. That ancient jealousy. She took a pause. A deep breath.

"Maureen?"

"Harold, I don't think I can talk about Queenie and her garden. I know I said I wanted to come here. But I was wrong. It's been a wasted journey. We just need to forget the whole thing."

Even as she said it, she knew it was not true. It might be possible for Harold to forget but for her there was no such way out. She might forget her entire life story. She might forget the dogs that attacked her and her father because she had not listened to him, even though he later bore the blame, and she might forget the humiliation of not getting into university or the beret that she subsequently threw away. She might forget seeing Harold for the first time as he danced like a madman and she watched transfixed, knowing her life had changed and there was no going back. She might even—God help her—somehow lose her most recent mistakes, but she would always see Queenie's monuments to Harold and David. Because they were beautiful. As much as she didn't want to, Maureen knew it. She knew it so deeply it was seared into her bones. Queenie had taken them both and rendered them beautiful while all Maureen had managed was a vacant bedroom and a tablet with little green stones. Surely it wasn't too much to ask that you get to the end, and looking back, you don't fill with horror and bitterness at all the things you got wrong. The mistakes you made, over and over, like falling repeatedly down the same old hole.

"Are you still there?"

"I'm still here," she said.

"You seem quiet."

"I'm tired. That's all."

"Did you get on well with Kate?"

"I told you already. I didn't stay long." She pursed her mouth. Changed the subject. "Did you eat?"

"When?"

"Today."

"Yes. We ate very well."

Another pause. Another not knowing what to say. "Well. Good night, then, Harold."

"Good night."

It seemed to Maureen that in the space of two days she had aged ten years. She felt ancient and ruined and empty.

———⸗———

It was a sleepless night. The third in a row. More like hovering above the surface of repose. She lay there, wide-eyed and restless, a prisoner of her own thoughts, alert to every creak in the radiator and alien banging of a door. It reminded her of the months following David's death when to give in to sleep had felt like a betrayal, and she had spent hours in his room, cocooned within his blue curtain, refusing to believe what she knew to be true. But she must have dozed in the end because she came to hearing wind beating at the window, and had no idea where she was. Red numbers were floating in the dark, telling her the time was 05:17. She knew something had happened that made the world different, but she didn't know what it was until she felt the blanket on top of her and knew with a fresh influx of pain that she had driven to Embleton Bay to find David in Queenie's Garden and ease something inside her, like taking out a splinter, yet what she had found had only filled her with hundreds more spikes.

It was no use. She couldn't sleep. She switched on the lamp and reached for her crossword puzzle, but all she could think about was the garden. Her eyes felt gritty and tight, and her head was a clamp. "Not the saddest thing," she heard Karen the volunteer saying, as she pointed to the holed piece of driftwood. "But one of them."

Maureen recalled the way Queenie had looked at her all those years ago as she pegged out her washing. Demeaning and full of pity. A chill went right through her. She threw on her clothes, ramming her arms into her coat and her feet into her shoes, barely pausing to switch off the lamp, pulling her suitcase out of the room, even though the silly wheels got stuck on the meeting point between the carpet and the landing, and she had to yank it. She looked for the receptionist in her booth but all the lights were off, so she placed her room key beside the toy palm tree and pulled open the front door.

Maureen couldn't leave that guesthouse fast enough.

11

ANNA DUPREE

Rage. Oh, such rage. Like a blazing column in her chest. How dare Queenie? How dare she? Maureen had not felt this way since the book group. The moon was a silver-white fragment, flooding the land in cold light. She followed the path of her own shadow, her driving shoes stumbling over the sand. Ahead, the skin of the sea heaved and waves rolled out of the dark. A salt smell pricked her nose and the wind came at her face. The noise was terrible. She crossed to the end of the bay and made her way up the steep wood steps, grasping at marram grass, but it burned her hands and that hurt too. She moved past the closed-up chalets toward the garden. Her car was parked at the golf course, ready to go, with her suitcase and handbag. Queenie could do whatever she liked for other people, she could even take Harold if she must, but she could not have Maureen's son. She could not have David.

In the dark, the garden was transformed. Things generally became smaller once you knew them but moonlight shone among the driftwood figures, magnifying each one. The wind made sounds she did not know, hissing and seething, followed briefly by silence. Maureen felt her way between the sculptures. A flutter of something caught her hand and she flinched. All around her rose the statues and pieces of driftwood and she was frightened, as if they were watching. She needed to get this over and done with. She needed to hurry.

Maureen moved toward the figure that she knew now to be her son. She placed her hands firmly on either side of the V-shape, as though grasping a pair of horns, and she pulled. Nothing happened. The wood slipped through her fingers, grazing them. She tried again. Same thing. If only she had gloves.

"Okay," she said. "Well, if that's what you want."

This time she stooped right over, cradling him beneath her so that the V-shape was either side of her body and she was at the very middle, and she wrenched yet again, really hard, but her balance wasn't right. Instead of freeing him, she lost her grip again and this time she stumbled backward. The ground seemed to shoot away from beneath her, sending her down. She heard a sharp crack and experienced an unforgiving pain. Oh, God, she thought. Please let it not be my son.

It took moments to work out what had happened. Moments that didn't flow from one another but happened in a more staccato way like a series of full stops. Everything was in the wrong

place. She was on her back. Sky. She was looking up at the
night sky. Stars, tiny and flickering. Something had slammed
against the back of her neck. The vertebrae of her spine felt
numb. She tried to breathe. It hurt. She stopped. She moved
what might be her leg. It *was* her leg. That hurt, too. She
couldn't be sure she still had toes. She tried to move and heard
a noise like an animal stuck underground and realized it was
coming from herself. She stopped trying to sit. She stayed lying
still. She took one breath. She took another. She was beginning
to feel cold.

"Maureen," she said. "Move."

But she couldn't. She couldn't move her arms or her feet or
her head because the moment she tried, there it was, astonishing pain in her neck. Suddenly all she wanted was to close her
eyes and sleep.

"Maureen," she said again, louder this time. "Move, you fool.
Move."

It was no good. She could be as impatient with herself as she
liked, but it made no difference. She couldn't do this. She was
in too much pain.

"Help!" she called. "Help!" Nothing answered or arrived.

The driftwood figure that was Harold was only a few feet
away. Maureen shuffled toward it, bit by bit, still on her back.
Her body seemed to be made of fragile pieces that were badly
put together. Keeping her neck rigid, she tried to reach for the
wooden structure, but sparks of pain stopped her. If she didn't
move her neck, she could do it. She rolled over. She clung on
with one arm, then the other, dragging herself to her knees, all
the while not moving her neck, holding it as if it were welded

to her shoulder blades, then crawling herself upward, until she managed to stand. She leaned her body against the driftwood piece. If she as much as twitched a muscle in her neck, the pain flashed.

There was nothing to do but wait for daylight. She stayed with her spine pressed against Harold because without him she knew she would fall apart, like a pile of stones, and she tried to imagine him behind her as she washed the dishes at the kitchen sink, but it was no good. She was caught in the very middle of Queenie's Garden, like a living relic, while the figures and statues watched her and whispered. All she could think of was the night in the bookshop.

Had she known? Did some part of her head know what was going to happen even when she bought her ticket for the event? "Oh. Don't you just *love* that book?" the bookshop owner said, and she pressed it to her chest as if it were attached to her vital organs. No. Maureen did not love that book. Reading it for her new book group, she had felt so wounded—she had no idea where to place herself. It was a story about a woman whose twenty-year-old son hanged himself. The only reason she finished the damn thing was because she wanted to be part of a book group. Otherwise she would have flung it out of the window. It was a vile book.

On the night, the shop was packed. Maureen chose a place at the end of a row, wanting to be alone, but an assistant asked last minute if she wouldn't mind moving in case there were latecomers. She had squeezed past other people to a seat in the

very middle, and her new acquaintances from the book group—
Deborah, Alice, and so on—were smiling at her in a polite way
from their rows. Maureen's heart felt tight, as if someone had
wound it in plastic bands. She was finding it hard to breathe.

To her surprise, the writer was even younger than she expected. She might only have been in her late twenties, wearing
a leopard-print dress, a pair of cowboy boots and a wide belt
that accentuated how neat and small she was. She turned to
the audience and the first thing she did was bow her head with
her hands clasped in prayer. Oh, Maureen hated this safari/
cowgirl writer.

Throughout the evening, she had a strange feeling of not
being there, as if she were dreaming, or as if she was remembering a bookshop from a dream. Her heart still felt com-
pressed, while strangely the rest of her body felt emptied.
Almost without any bones at all. The writer spoke about the
book and her life, and gave some observations about grief that
made the room go silent. The bookshop owner said this had
been the most important and moving interview of her life, and
after that there were questions from the audience. Someone
asked whether the writer believed in God, and the writer said
she believed in what we could not see, and the audience nodded and a few wept. All the while Maureen remained absolutely still, both present and somehow not there at all. Then a
woman in the audience put up her hand and said, "What I
want to ask . . ."

A shuffling of chairs. Rows of faces turning, wary, confused.
The owner saying she was sorry, but no one could hear, and a
young man with a mic now wriggling past knees to get to

Maureen. Because she was the woman in the audience with her hand in the air. She was the one whose legs were shaking as she took to her feet and whose voice was too shrill—but at the same time it did not seem to be her.

"What I want to ask, Anna Dupree, is how dare you?"

Maureen could no longer recall her exact words. The memory was a series of stains on her mind, as if a shutter had come down between the place in her brain where words formed and the other where they took on meaning. She was rigid, on the edge of a void. She knew she had asked if Anna Dupree had ever lost a child, if she really thought she knew what that was like, when look at her, she was barely old enough to have a baby, let alone a full-grown adult son. She asked exactly what right she had to write about something she did not know and sell millions of copies all over the world to other people who did not know either. Had she called Anna Dupree a tourist? Probably. Had she accused everyone else in the bookshop of being a tourist? Chances were, yes, she'd done that too. Now she had started speaking she didn't feel able to stop, though stop she must, but to stop would mean there would be consequences, there would be the terrible thing that must happen next after a woman says something like this, so she kept plowing on, closer and closer to the void. A member of the book group with pretty hoop earrings had shaken her head, as if to say, No, no, Maureen, please don't do this to yourself.

Meanwhile Anna Dupree listened with her hand to her mouth. Her face looked stretched.

Maureen wanted to leave. More specifically, she wanted not to have come in the first place. She wanted none of this to have happened but she was stuck in the middle of the shop, in a jungle of fold-up chairs and kind people who were doing their best to look elsewhere, with her face so red she could feel it burning, and she wanted to say, I am sorry, I did not mean this, but she had already said it. It was too late. Besides. She did mean it. That was the trouble. She really did. Every terrible word.

A difficult child.

She made her way to the door, crushing her knees into the backs of chairs, pushing past people's elbows and shoulders and, as she hit the warm air of the summer evening, she over-heard someone murmur, "Yes, that's his *wife*," and she knew they were talking about her and Harold. She knew she would never come back to the bookshop. She knew that when emails came about the book group, she would feel so conflicted that she would delete them without a first glance. She didn't want to pick up another damn book, not ever. She knew, too, that people would move away from her in the supermarket—even though Harold would say she was only imagining that, which irritated her because it made her sound paranoid. She would shop online instead.

A few months later, Maureen read an interview in a Sunday magazine where Anna Dupree talked about her worldwide bestselling book and how she was going to stop writing fiction because of something a reader had said to her. *I realized I could not make it up any more.* Maureen buried the magazine in the recycling bin. "Serves you right," she said. But she no longer knew if she was talking to herself or Anna Dupree.

It was not the worst thing, what she had done that night,

just as the unnamed figure in Queenie's Garden was not the saddest. But it was worse than a leaking bladder, worse even than falling as you tried to steal something from a garden, because Maureen had laid her deepest loss at the feet of the world and experienced nothing but an affirmation of her left-outness and her shame. David's loss was her secret. It was the rock against which she was forever shattered. And Maureen was a loose cannon, firing herself in all directions. She was sundered from life, irrevocably and completely. She would never be free.

At first light, Maureen shuffled her way through the garden. The figures and sculptures were barely shadows. She could just about walk if she didn't move her neck but any slight turn of her head sent pain shooting down her arms. The rising sun gave orange and pink flashes and the sea held its light and so did an inlet of water winding its passage through the sand. The beach was littered with kelp, their roots like knuckles, and driftwood, and plastic bottles. She felt weak. She couldn't remember when she had last eaten. In the distance, sunlight struck the windows of the line of houses of Embleton, and briefly they flamed. She longed to speak to Harold but he would be asleep and, anyway, she had no idea how to explain what she had been trying to do. She didn't even know how to get into the car.

In the end Maureen lowered herself, piece by piece. She started the engine, and inched the car at a snail's pace away from the bay. She could manage if she didn't look down at the pedals or the gear stick, though she couldn't move her neck either to check her rearview mirror. All those years of holding her head high and now it was doing it all by itself. She concentrated on the road ahead, forcing herself to stay awake, but the pain was coming in wheeling patterns that made her drowsy. She knew she should turn round and drive back but she could not bear another night in that guesthouse. She heard the roar of a van behind, too close. As he overtook, the driver swore and shouted at her to get off the road.

It was too much. She couldn't do it. She didn't even know where she was going. The truth was, she could go where she liked, but she would never get away from herself. Because it wasn't Anna Dupree she hated. Not really. It wasn't even her damn book, or the many people who loved it. It was the fact that this young woman had been able to conjure something beautiful out of grief, while Maureen, who lived and breathed it like a full-time professional, could not. And now she knew Queenie had found a way to do the same with her garden.

Maureen pulled over at the next garage and rang the only person she could think of.

12

COFFEE BEANS

"Maureen? What happened?"

Kate was calling Maureen's name even as she lowered her foot out of the driver's door and bundled down from the truck. Her granddaughter Maple was in the passenger seat, sitting on her mother's lap. They had parked right up close to Maureen at the garage.

"I can't move."

"Where does it hurt?"

"I don't know. My neck. Everywhere."

"Will you let me help?"

Maureen felt Kate's hands reaching toward her and asking, "Okay? Okay?" as she began lifting her gently out of the car. What was happening did not feel right but she let Kate help her while she also wondered where she should put her hands.

She didn't want to push her away but neither could she hold her arms around Kate so she just left them dangling in mid-air. Kate was smiling but Maureen had no idea if it was for her and she still had no idea what to say. She noticed Kate's hands were warm and very strong. She guided Maureen carefully toward the truck and flung open the rear door, while still holding Maureen, and supported her as she took the steps, one at a time, all the while saying, "Okay? Okay?" From there she shuffled Maureen right to the back of the truck, where the bed was already pulled out. In the passenger seat, Maple turned to watch, her eyes very dark and round over her mother's shoulder, as Kate guided Maureen's body on top of the eiderdown and lifted her feet. It was so good to be lying down. Maureen kept herself rigid. She closed her eyes. I could die now, she thought. Truly, I am done.

"Is that lady going to hospital?" she heard Maple ask.

"We're going to look after her," said her mother. "We have to be quiet."

Kate's face was so close, Maureen could feel her breath. It smelled of something like toothpaste and earth. Maureen kept her eyes shut as she heard Kate's voice saying, "Okay, darlin'. This is what we're going to do. Sarah is going to drive your car back to the camp before she goes to work. I'm going to take you to the hospital and get you checked out and after that you can rest with me. You don't have to say anything."

She was speaking to Maureen slowly, and even though she was so close, her voice sounded as if it were a long way off. Maureen kept her eyes closed. She gave the softest of murmurs to show she had understood but she didn't move and neither was she ready to reply. She wanted to stay very still like this, being spoken to kindly as if she were a child, while deep down the waves of pain pushed through her.

Maureen felt something firm on her head and realized it must be Kate's hand, touching her short white hair. "You've had a hard time, but it's okay now. You don't have to go any-where until you're ready. You're going to be fine."

Her neck was not broken, but the muscles were sprained, her back was badly bruised and her blood pressure was too low. Maureen needed to rest for a few days and limit her move-ment. She certainly wasn't fit to drive. Kate had waited with her at the hospital. She held Maple on her lap and read stories, over and over again, while Maureen sat ramrod-straight beside her, wishing someone would stuff a baking tray against her spine, not daring to move unless she shifted her entire body, not even daring to speak. She had forgotten how children could listen to the same story and find something endlessly comforting in the repetition of it.

"Are you in pain?" the nurse asked.

"I can manage," she said.

He smiled as if he knew better and gave her the first of a course of strong painkillers. He showed her some exercises to ease her neck and shoulders.

"You were lucky, Mrs. Fry," he said. She did not ask what he meant by that because she knew he was right.

Kate said she had rung Harold to explain that Maureen had taken a fall but was going to be okay if she rested for a few days. She had reassured him Maureen was not seriously hurt and there was no need for him to come because Kate would look after her. "He wants to say hello," she said, and she rang his number again and held the phone against Maureen's ear.

"Oh, Maw," she heard him say. All that love in his voice. "Oh, sweetheart."

And she nodded, and said, "Uh, uh, uh," because that was the only thing she could do without hurting.

"Are you okay? Will you be okay?"

She said, "Uh uh uh," again.

"Shall I come?"

"No," she said. "It okay. Kate here." The drugs were kicking in.

Afterward she allowed Kate to guide her back into the truck and already she felt she knew a little more of the way Kate held her, so she trusted her to take her weight. Kate drove them slowly to the camp, then heated a pan of soup that they ate at the table. Maureen was so exhausted she could barely lift the spoon to her mouth. Kate fetched the eiderdown and helped her get underneath it. The bed no longer felt lumpy or alien. Kate pulled the eiderdown right up to Maureen's chin and said, "There, there, darlin'," until Maureen's eyelids drooped. Sleep came suddenly. Maybe it was the painkillers. She was aware she was thinking of Harold and wanting to speak to him again but couldn't summon the energy to open her eyes.

When Maureen woke, she felt she was coming up from somewhere like a black hole. She wasn't sure why she was there, or even where "there" was. And then she made out Kate in the wing-back chair reading a library book under a lamp and wearing a pair of big glasses. Briefly Maureen was alarmed, as if she had been absent for some time, during which things might have happened that she didn't know, and she tried to sit up, but the pain was too much and she stayed lying down.

"Rest," said Kate, glancing up once from her book. "I've spoken to Harold again. He sends you all his love. He's with Rex."

"Did he say what they were doing?" said Maureen. She closed her eyes before Kate answered.

When she next woke, Maple was curled in Kate's lap and Kate was reading her another story, but her voice was low, more like a chant, and Maureen couldn't make out the words. She didn't need to: it was a comfort just hearing them, and not being alone. She pulled Kate's eiderdown over her head and fell asleep once more. The next time she woke it was morning and the sky was a band of silver beneath purple cloud. The truck was empty.

Kate brought coffee on a tray and arranged two cups on the table. She helped Maureen sit and gave her cushions and another painkiller. They successfully avoided talking about what had happened during her previous visit and spoke instead about inconsequential things, like coffee. Kate told Maureen she ground her own beans and Maureen said she always bought instant powder and Kate paused and said, with steeled intensity, that no one should drink that crap. It was full of shit, she said, you might as well as drink washing-up water. She served her own coffee from a silver pot that looked like something you would find in a Turkish bazaar and she poured it into two small blue cups, like a ritual. Maureen managed one sip—she couldn't move her neck enough for more—and found what Kate had said to be true. It was the most delicious coffee. Hot and milky with only a hint of bitterness; a sweetness of chocolate, too. And this way they sidestepped their differences to move forward.

"Shall I lift the cup for you?" said Kate.

"You don't have to. I can manage."

"Oh, Maureen, why won't you let another woman help you for once?"

So she lifted the coffee toward Maureen's mouth and placed the saucer beneath Maureen's chin and this time she took a good proper drink.

"I feel I owe you an apology," Maureen said.

Kate smiled. "You don't owe me anything. But I'm glad you rang me, Maureen, when you needed help. I'm glad you gave us another chance."

When their cups were empty, they sat for a while not saying anything until Kate reached for Maureen's hand and spread her own firmly around it and kept it over Maureen's so that she could feel its weight and the calluses on her palms. Kate said, without looking at Maureen, but toward the window: "How do we do it? How do we accept the unacceptable?"

After the quiet, her voice filled the room and so did the question. It came over Maureen how tired she was, as if it was evening again instead of morning. Kate closed the curtains. "Can I get you anything else?"

"No, thank you. You've helped me more than enough."

"I'll let you rest."

In the dimmed light, Maureen lay under Kate's eiderdown and fell into another deep sleep.

—— # ——

Later, Kate knocked on the door of the truck and asked if
Maureen was feeling any better. She had a favor to ask. She
and her daughter had a women's meeting to go to—it would
only take two hours. She wondered if Maureen would let
Maple sit with her. "I don't know, Maureen. I feel bad about
asking. I just wondered if you'd think about it."

Maureen said, "Yes. I'm glad you asked."

"Do you think you could manage?"

"Maybe. I'm not sure Maple likes me."

At this Kate laughed. "Oh, Maureen," she said. "Listen to
yourself for once. She's a child. If you're kind to her, she'll like
you."

Before Kate left, Maple brought her book and coloring pencils into the truck. Kate had put on red lipstick that Maureen
wasn't sure about but she held her tongue and said nothing.
Maple hugged her grandmother hard, hanging from her neck
like another vast necklace, and Maureen began to think the
whole plan would not work, but Kate kissed her and said Maureen was a good woman and then goodbye. To begin with,
Maple was wary of Maureen. She sat at the table but kept her
arms around her book and her things, as if she feared Maureen
might steal them. The best thing was to give her some space.

Maureen made her way to the kitchenette and washed a few
plates. These are very good painkillers, she thought. She found
a cloth and ran hot soapy water into the plastic sink.

From the table, Maple began to talk. She was still coloring
in, but she went on without stopping, speaking about whatever

came into her mind, with no need for Maureen to remark on any of it, though she listened to everything Maple said, entranced, because it was so long since she'd been alone with a child like this. She had forgotten how they could talk and talk. She spoke about a girl who was her friend and a black-and-white dog that barked on the farm as well as her bicycle and so many other things, none joined together except in the sweet place that was Maple's head. Then the little girl slipped down from her stool at the table and carried it to Maureen's side and asked if she could see what Maureen was doing.

Without moving her neck, Maureen helped Maple stand on her stool and let her swish her hands in the soapy water and wash a few spoons, with Maple still chattering away, until Maureen realized she was no longer listening to the words, only the tune of them, because she was wiping everything in the vicinity. She was wiping the taps, the rim of the plastic sink, and the lip where it met the draining-board, the unit surfaces, the pots of utensils, the kettle, and the splashback behind it. She was even scouring the dirt from the plug and the knobs on the drawers, and the hooks for the tea-towels. She worked on, calmed by the cloth in warm water, the rinse and squeeze, calmed by Maple's sing-song voice, but most of all calmed by the experience of those surfaces becoming uniformly clean—even though there was no disinfectant spray, and no canister of Pledge or Mr. Sheen, and no rubber gloves either. She tidied the mugs, arranging them with the handles pointing all to the right. Already she felt exhausted. Then Maple got down and lay on the bed and asked Maureen to read her picture book.

It was about rabbits. Rabbits who lived in a house, not even a burrow, and wore hats and coats. Three pages in, Maureen was falling asleep. But Maple called her name and Maureen felt an old crease of pleasure, hearing her name spoken by a child, "Maw-weeeen." It sounded so sticky and exact. So she went back to the book and managed another page—the rabbits appeared to be making soup—before closing her eyes, until this time she stretched out beside Maple and fell asleep.

When Kate and her daughter returned, the old woman and the child were both lying on top of the bed. Maureen was snoring loudly, her mouth wide, and Maple was also open-mouthed and flush-cheeked, tucked into the crook of Maureen's arm. Sarah lifted Maple and Kate moved an extra cushion closer to Maureen. She left a packet of painkillers and a glass of water in case Maureen needed them when she woke.

In the morning, Maureen asked if she could take another look at Maple's picture book. She wanted to know how it ended.

"That was quite a good story," she said. "I liked it."

There. The nice words just came out.

13

MOONLIGHT SONATA

It was a long time since anyone had looked after Maureen. She stayed for three more days in the cave-like truck that was filled with dream-catchers and Buddha statues and chakra stones and rose lamps, and smelled of incense. Kate made meals and washed her clothes, and when Maureen looked out of the window, she saw her comfortable slacks flapping on the washing line beside Maple's little clothes. She watched the girl riding on her bicycle or playing with her mother with her rainbow hair. Sometimes she watched the other women, stopping to talk to one another outside, or sharing a coffee. Occasionally Maple curled up next to Maureen with one of her books, and Maureen would manage to hold her neck upright enough to read to her. The outside world was contained by that one window, sometimes dawn-pale, sometimes cloudy, sometimes hidden by the curtain. She slept in a way she had never slept before, deep and free, looking at the clock and no longer knowing if it was morning or evening, but closing her eyes and sleeping again. She phoned Harold often and he told her the things he was doing with Rex, which were the same things they always did—playing drafts and watching for birds. She asked if they were remembering to eat properly, and he told her, yes, they were doing splendidly, they had finished a goulash and a stew, but they still had a pie left, and a soup. The thing he wanted most, he kept saying, was for her to get better.

"I'm glad you're with Kate," he told her on the third day. "I knew you'd like her. Of all the people I walked with she was my favorite. Did I ever tell you that?"

"Well," said Maureen, "maybe you did. But I like hearing it again."

"I miss you."

"I miss you too."

"But you'll be home soon."

"Tomorrow, I hope."

"Guess what?"

"I don't know."

"We saw a black redstart."

"That's a bird, is it?"

"Yes, Maw. It's like you. It's a beauty."

That night, Maureen opened her eyes and knew she had been woken by the slight noise of a door. The curtains were open and the room was lit by the moon, as bright as daylight, but everything luminous and slightly blue.

There he was, watching her from the wing-back chair. He had placed her clothes on the floor, carefully, though, so as not to crumple them.

"David," she whispered.

"Hello," he said.

He was sitting the way he used to, legs sprawled, like a tall person inside a body that had grown too small. He was wearing his old greatcoat with the wide lapels that were pinned all over with badges, and his favorite black boots. His hair was long and thick and brown, just as it had been before he shaved his head. He looked the way he always looked, which meant that he was a little disheveled and roughed up around the edges, but there was a sharpness to his eyes. He wasn't high or drunk or anything. He was holding a winter bouquet of twigs that looked like witch hazel and scarlet dogwood, along with some fern and ivy berries and crimson haws. His fingernails were green.

"Is it really you? Is it really my son?"

"It's me."

"I began to think I would never see you again."

"Well," he said. Two or three times he shrugged in a bashful way. "Here I am."

He was quiet for a while, just watching her with those beautiful dark eyes, and she remained in stillness too, not wanting to do anything that would break the moment. She wondered if the winter twigs might be for her or just something he happened to be carrying.

"Are you all right?" she said at last.

"I'm all right."

"Is that a mad thing to say?"

"I don't think so."

"There was a time I used to talk to you. I talked to you all the time. I talked more to you than anyone else and that's the truth." She was speaking softly, rapidly, afraid the words would dry up if she didn't get them out. "I told you everything. About what I was doing and what I was thinking and you listened. You were so patient with me. I know I'm not being clear. I wish I could explain it to you. Maybe I don't need to."

He nodded. Then he looked down at the bouquet and touched a seed head of old man's beard, which was soft and white, like a wispy ball of thread.

"In the end I stopped. I stopped talking to you. Did it hurt you that I stopped? Should I have kept talking? Would you have liked that?"

"It's okay."

"I know. I know. I'm asking too many questions. It's just seeing you again. There's so much I want to say."

He lodged the bouquet beneath his arm and reached for a cigarette from his pocket. He lit it with a match, and the smoke turned from gray to blue as it hit a shaft of moon from the window. He said, "Did something happen to your neck?"

"Oh. It's nothing."

"It looks like it hurts."

"I'm taking pills. I sleep a lot. I'm a bit drugged up."

He smiled and gave a long pull on his cigarette, squinting slightly as he exhaled.

"There is a woman here. She's looking after me. I thought I didn't like her but I was wrong. Kate is a good woman. So I'm fine, honestly. I'm just stuck for a few days. Holed up. Isn't that what people say?"

She was afraid that if she stopped talking, he would disappear. God help her, already he seemed less present.

"I don't know. I don't know what people would say. I was never very good at all that."

"David?" she said. "If I stayed here longer, would you stay too?"

He smiled again, but this time as if she was asking something too painful to answer, and then rubbed his eyes with his knuckle. She remembered how as a child he would rub them while he did his homework until his face flamed and his knees would twitch, and how she would worry that learning the way he did, ferociously like that, and wanting to excel, was a kind of punishment. And she remembered then how she had wanted the same when she was young. How she had wanted to be more than the place she came from. They were the same, the two of them. David had only taken up the thing that she started.

"I wish I'd got you a dog."

"A dog?"

"Yes. But I was frightened. Of dogs, I mean. The farmer let his dogs chase me when I was small. But you always wanted a dog."

"I don't remember."

"You went on and on about a dog."

"Ha," he said. "Did I?"

"Don't you remember the dog we gave you for Christmas?"

"What dog?"

"Oh, it was a hideous thing that went woof. You kept it in the box."

He laughed again and now she laughed too, and it was so good to be laughing again with David. They had always understood each other.

She said, "I saw Queenie's Garden. Did you?"

"Why would I have seen her garden?"

"I don't know. I'm coming to the conclusion I know very little. I'm a silly old woman. That's all I know." She thought of the emptiness that was still inside her, even after all these years. Now that she was with him at last, she did not know how she could bear to give him up. "Oh, David. I can't move on. I'm sorry. I'm thinking of myself. I don't want a life without you. Don't leave me again. Stay."

He flinched as if she had struck him. She had said too much. Yet again her mouth had gone and said completely and utterly the wrong thing. Her damn mouth. And this time it wasn't to a stranger, it was to her own son.

David slid off the chair and put down his bouquet and sat hunched on the floor, with his chin against his knees. She had thought the bouquet must have been tied together with string but it wasn't, and now the twigs and flowers had fallen apart. It didn't look like a proper bouquet any more but instead a bunch of winter things he might have snapped off in passing because he liked the look of them. Or maybe he hadn't even given it a thought. Maybe his hands had just snapped off the twigs for something to do.

He began to cry but very quietly into his arms, rocking himself, as though he didn't want her to know what he was doing.

Maureen got off the bed and sank on her knees beside him and lifted her arm around his shoulders, pulling him close until he leaned the full force of his weight against hers. Her shoulder gave a twist but that was nothing. You can twist yourself right inside out, she thought, but I will stay put. His hair was soft on her cheek and smelled of the shampoo he had used as a teenager; a slightly medical smell. He had seen an advert for it on the television and gone on and on at her to buy it. It was years since she'd smelled it or even thought of it, yet now it felt the most real thing in her life, more real even than the floor she was kneeling on or the moonlight at the window. She wanted to get the smell right inside her so that she would never forget it. She thought of the many things she wanted to say. *I missed so much. How could I have let you go?* She wanted to be able to buy him that shampoo he loved and ask in the mornings how he had slept, and cook him an egg the way he liked it, sunny side up, and understand what he had meant as a boy when he'd said he wanted to be the world's guest.

But none of this did she say because he got there first. He asked if she could just listen. He had things he needed to tell her because he knew they were in his way but they were such terrible things. He kept saying, "Sorry, sorry, sorry." Almost every other word was an apology.

"It's okay," she said. "It's okay. You can tell me, son. I'm here. Of course I'll listen. You tell me whatever you want to say. Tell me everything. I'm not going anywhere."

He told her he used to steal money from her purse all the

time, and he was so sorry about that. He wished he had not got into drinking and the pills but it was only because he had believed for a while he could be something special, and he needed to quieten the voice in his head that was saying he was no one. He said he remembered running into the sea at Bantham Beach when he was a boy and he didn't know why he had kept running, except that he thought he could swim, and he was sorry for that, and he was sorry, too, for the day he'd graduated when he'd kept them waiting two hours in the hot sun so they missed the whole ceremony.

And Maureen said, "I know, I know. It's okay, son. It's okay. But, oh, my lord, you are not no one. Do you hear me?"

He told her the truth was that he hadn't actually finished his course at Cambridge, he had been sent down, so the whole graduation thing was a lie, and he was a shit because she had bought a dress and Harold had bought a jacket, and they were so proud of him. He had watched them, he said, from a distance, and now he felt sick to think what that must have been like for them, waiting in their best clothes.

"I know," she said. "It's okay. And, anyway, that was one terrible dress I wore that day. I don't know what I was thinking of. Really. I looked like a boiled shrimp. *I* would have stood me up."

He said he wished he had never shaved his head because he knew how much that pained her. He said did she remember the hat he loved with a feather in it, and she laughed and said, "Oh, yes, son. Yes, I remember that hat. That was such a fine hat. So *dandy*. You were a peacock in that hat. It's okay, son. I know, I know. It's okay."

There was so much more he wanted to tell her. He couldn't unburden himself fast enough. She had barely taken hold of one thing, and he was handing her another, yet everything he said chimed with something that was buried inside her. He said how much he loved his first pair of shoes when he was three ("I know, I know"), and did she remember the bonsai tree he tried to grow, and she said, yes, as she held him. "It's okay, son. I know, I know. It's okay."

She drew him closer. When they were standing, she barely used to reach his shoulders, but she spread herself wide around him. I would become the size of the world for this boy, she thought. Then she brushed back his hair and lifted his face toward hers, but already it was lapsing away, his dark eyes more blurred and even his shoulders a little thinner. "You are some-one," she said. "Do you hear? Goodness me, you are someone."

She stayed at his side, listening and holding him, though she could no longer make out the words, and later she heard the first birdsong and found she was lying in the bed. The truck was empty. The curtains were drawn. She was wearing her nightdress. David was not sitting in the wing-back chair and she was not beside him and there was no winter bouquet. There was no sign whatsoever that he had been there, not even a smell of shampoo or sprinkling of cigarette ash. Her clothes were folded on the arm of the chair, just as she'd left them.

She lay on the bed, as the sun came up and filled the truck with winter light, and the birds kept calling, *Tchink tchink, Haw haw haw! Tsee tsee!* Good morning! Good morning!

14

WINTER BOUQUET

After she left Kate, Maureen did something she did not understand. She drove into Hexham and asked a stranger where she might find a bookshop. She bought a copy of Anna Dupree's paperback, and then she found a florist and chose a winter bouquet. She did not understand but she still went and did those things. After all, they were only two more in a whole journey of things she did not understand. She put them on the passenger seat, and drove back to the golf course. She carried them to Queenie's Garden for her third and final visit.

Her parting with Kate had been affectionate and slow. Maureen had not spoken about her night but she believed Kate might have sensed something, without fully knowing what it was, as she straightened the wing-back chair and paused a moment to smooth a ruck in the upholstery. She helped Maureen pack her suitcase and made one of her pots of coffee, which they drank in their coats on the plastic chairs outside. She gave Maureen a bag of freshly ground beans to take home for Harold, and they promised to keep in touch and see one another again. Then, to Maureen's surprise and pleasure, Kate had taken Maureen's face between her palms and kissed it with a completeness that reminded her of putting a stamp on a letter. "I won't forget you lying in my truck," she said. "Whatever happens, I will always keep that memory of you here."

By the time she was walking past the golf course toward the dunes it was already midafternoon, though the sun had broken through and lit the land crosswise, throwing long, spindly shadows, and catching a nearby cloud, so that it glowed like a tangerine above the bay. There was only one other person in the garden—a man sitting in the far corner—dressed in a robe under an anorak and hat, his head bowed, holding prayer beads. There was rain in the air, but only light. It wouldn't hurt her.

Maureen made her way past Harold's driftwood sculpture, and David's, toward the unnamed one with a hole for a heart. She found a good place for the book beside a statue made of bottle tops and corks, with an additional garland of bright pink paper flowers, and she laid it there.

"I hope you write another blockbuster, Anna Dupree," she said. "I really do. But I hope you don't mind if I don't read it."

She turned now to the holed piece of driftwood that people believed had no name. Because it was Maureen. She knew it. She had known it since that night in the guesthouse. She knelt and placed her hand where the hole was, and for a moment it was full again. The hurt was gone. Her anger too, and her resentment. At last they were not there. She had been wrong: this brittle piece of driftwood was not an act of unkindness on Queenie's part, or even pity. It was one of forgiveness. Queenie had understood Maureen's grief that day they'd met beside the washing line, and done the best she could to give it a place, just as Maureen now knew her letter for Harold had been a letting go of love. She was glad she had kept it in a shoebox. Without any exchange of words, they had taken up each other's loss, and given meaning to what was unbearable.

Maureen remained kneeling, all alone in that garden she did not understand. Once again there was a rip-split in the cloud and the light shone down on the sea, catching flecks of rain, so that the air was filled with specks of snow-white brightness. A kestrel breasted the sea wind and hung, wings hooked. Maureen watched it for so long she suddenly felt able to see as far as the bird saw, and beyond.

All of Northumberland stretched away, swelling and wimpling toward the south—over the patchwork of low hills and plains, flint walls, patterns of fields, the valleys and fells, over the Cheviot Hills, the backbone of the Pennines, the limestone gorges of the Peak District, the western velvet spur of the Forest of Bowland, the Yorkshire Dales, the rolling Cotswolds, the Mendips, the chalk coasts, the mighty rivers, Tyne, Ouse, Trent, Thames, Exe, the wetlands, forests and woods, the trees that were so various they appeared beneath her like moss and algae, the network of roads and railways and canals, the factories and warehouses, the sprawling cities, the sewage works and toxic heaps, the asbestos, the plastic, the landfill—all the way to the heather-purple peaks of Dartmoor, and a blue estuary, and a road of little houses, each with a garden, where Harold gazed up at the sky, watching for birds. She imagined the edges of the world shifting slowly and she stayed in its mysterious motion as her mind made windings deep into the earth through holes and runnels, where closely woven grasses hid the sky. She followed the ancient path of water and saw the curlicues of buried shells, she followed beetles into scrolls of leaves, and on and on, deeper and deeper, through to where larvae were buried, and she was no more than an eyeless globe in the dark, or a mantle of roots creeping out its threads. Then the kestrel dropped out of view, and once more she was in Queenie's Garden.

"Well," she said, coming to, "Maureen, Maureen. Now you've finally lost your marbles."

Maureen stared at all the driftwood sculptures and the seed heads like umbrellas. *I am the world's guest*, she thought. And suddenly she understood. She understood what David had meant when he was a boy. She had lived her life as if she was owed something extra because he had been taken away, and other women's sons had not. She thought of Harold watching for birds and how his face lit up when he saw a bluethroat. To have lived a whole life and then find wonder in a tiny creature covered with feathers, weighing no more than a coin. What was it all for, if not for that? She felt the painful shock of joy that floods in, like blood pushing into a limb that has been starved. It was about forgiveness, the whole story. Harold's pilgrimage and Queenie's letter, and now Maureen's winter journey too. The chimes and necklaces of stones moved in the wind and so did the seed heads. Yes, they said. Yes, Maureen! Everything was about that. She thought of all the strangers who had found a resting place for their losses that were too terrible to bear. The padlocks for love, the paper crosses, the photographs, the keys and flowers, homemade relics and hundreds of candles, the poems and messages. Forgive me, forgive me, for continuing to live when you are gone. The essential loneliness of people was there, wherever you cast your eye—it was in a service station, it was in a bookshop, it was in a parked car by the side of the road—so the things they did to try and bear the loss were choices that required respect. Such acts of love were only so many different ways of saying the same thing, because really there were no words to say.

Maureen got to her feet and laid her winter bouquet against the V-shaped monument. Queenie had been right to place David in her garden. He was not Maureen's lost son, he was himself. He belonged to no one but himself.

"Thank you, Queenie," she said, and she found, to her surprise, that she was weeping.

From the car park, Maureen rang Harold. She told him she would drive through the evening and be home very late, though she wanted to drop off a card for a night-security man who had been helpful near Exeter. To all this he said yes. Yes, of course, goodness, yes. She must drive carefully and stop whenever she needed. If she wanted to, she must find a place to sleep. He couldn't wait to see her, but the most important thing was that she was safe. Then she asked, "What have you two eaten today?"

"Oh, we've eaten like kings. Rex and I had sandwiches."

"What did you put inside?"

"The sandwiches?"

"Yes."

"I don't think we put anything inside them."

"So they were bread, then? Really they were bread."

"Yes," he said, laughing as if this was a happy new word he hadn't come across before. "Did you hear that, Rex? Our sandwiches were bread!"

Maureen took one last look across the bay toward Queenie's Garden. Brave things had been happening in the world, even though she hadn't noticed. Tiny black packages of buds on the branches and the smallest of shoots from the ground, as green as jewelry. The wind felt sharp and there was still a low ache in her neck, but she experienced no pain.

Maureen stayed a while longer, reluctant to give up the last of the day. Reluctant even to give up her solitude. It was so peaceful. In the distance, Queenie's Garden waved and sparkled. She watched the clouds frill with gold against the bracken-red sky, and the light that tipped upward in floods, even though the sun was no more than a lozenge on the horizon. A flock of tiny brown birds swooped down to a winter bush, chit-chattering away, like gossips on a street corner. What was it they were saying? Whatever it was, she liked it. So busy, so loud! *Tchink, tchink, Haw haw haw! Tsee, tsee! Choo choo!* She couldn't say how and, even if she could, she didn't need to, but she knew she was the happiest she had been in a long time.

"Maureen," she said quietly. "Maureen. Maureen."

Then she got into the car to make the journey home.

ACKNOWLEDGMENTS

A little over ten years ago, my first novel had the good fortune to fall into the hands of Susanna Wadeson, editor at Doubleday. Since then our book output has grown in size, and so has our friendship. My thanks are, as always, to Susanna for her faith, wisdom, questions and dedication, and for giving me the freedom to write about the things that move me. This book is for you.

Thank you to my wonderful agent, Clare Conville, and all at Conville & Walsh. Thank you to Hazel Orme and Kate Samano and the copy-editing team, Cat Hillerton in production, Beci Kelly in art, Emma Burton and Lilly Cox in marketing, Oli Grant in audio, Laura Ricchetti and Natasha Photiou in international sales, Tom Chicken, Laura Garrod, Emily Harvey, Neil Green and Elspeth Dougall in UK sales. Thank you to

Andrew Davidson for the exquisite illustrations. Thank you to Clio Seraphim and Kiara Kent and the entire Random House team. Thank you to those who championed Harold Fry all those years ago—Erica Wagner, David Headley, Cathy Retzenbrink, Fanny Blake—and have continued to be so generous over the years. Thank you for your unequivocal encouragement, Larry Finlay, and thank you, too, to Alison Barrow, because without your spark, guidance and friendship, none of this would be happening.

Thank you, as always, to my family, for your love. To Sarah Edghill, for casting an eye over an early draft of the first chapters of this book and having the courage to tell me it didn't work. (She was right. I started again.) Thank you to Niamh Cusack for reading every one of my stories over many years, even the ones that were emails.

Thank you to my husband, Paul Venables. In truth, the thank-you is a private one. But Paul has been involved with my writing from the very start and I couldn't do what I do without him. Sometimes it is good and right to shout about things like that.

Lastly, and above all, my thanks are both to the readers who have read with such kindness over the years—asking me questions that inspired more thinking, generously sharing their own stories—and the booksellers and librarians who kept getting books to us, even when we were all locked inside. The gate-keepers of reading. Where would we be without you?

MAUREEN

Rachel Joyce

A BOOK CLUB GUIDE

AN INTERVIEW WITH RACHEL JOYCE

Adapted from an original recording for BBC Radio 4's Bookclub program, presented by James Naughtie and recorded in 2021. One of over 300 interviews with the world's leading authors, from Isabel Allende, Donna Tartt and Margaret Atwood, to Colm Toibin and Colson Whitehead, which are all available to listen to on BBC Sounds.

Sometimes the simplest of stories are the most powerful.

The Unlikely Pilgrimage of Harold Fry is the story of a journey prompted by guilt and a sense of emotional incompleteness that does indeed become a pilgrimage. An act of homage by Harold to his friend Queenie, who's dying, and in truth, a quest for himself. Rachel Joyce's novel starts in the simplest way: a letter from Queenie tells Harold that she's dying. They had been workmates together. And so without planning it, Harold starts to walk from Kingsbridge in Devon to Berwick-upon-Tweed to see her. He begins simply by going from postbox to postbox, unable to decide whether he should post a letter and gradually finds himself drawn unexpectedly into the journey of a wanderer, walking the length of England and leaving everything behind, in particular his wife, Maureen, deeply unhappy and tormented by the absence of their only son David, who hovers, unseen, over the story. Maureen's emotions are the counterbalance to Harold's as they both reflect on their life together, their drifting apart, and, in their different ways, their search for peace. Readers have been captivated by this novel in vast numbers; there is something about Harold Fry: his innocence, the little guilty secrets underneath, his touching determination to finish his journey that turns him, like Maureen, into a friend we all seem to know.

Q: This is a journey of about 600 miles. Harold walks it. Are you a walker?
A: I'm an ambler. I'm a wanderer, actually. I'm the kind of person who sets off with not the right gear and often not really knowing where I'm really going.

Q: And so the idea of Harold almost drifting into this journey, which seems like a compulsive one, but nonetheless is one that's come about in a very unexpected way.
A: It's instinct, I think that's what it is. There are moments in life when you almost don't realize why you have to do something, but you know you have to do it, and I'd say this is one of those moments for Harold.

Q: I'd like to ask you how you got into Harold's mind. How easy or difficult was it to write from a male perspective as a female writer?

A: I actually found it really, really straightforward, partly because the book had started as a play on Radio 4, so I kind of knew Harold's voice really well. It had come to me really quickly and easily. Writing from his point of view was actually really liberating for me, to not be myself. I think Harold and share a few things. I realized early on that we were both doing a journey that we might not be able to make it to the end of, and that's great as a writer, especially when it's your first book, finding the similarities and parallels between you and the main character. And there was also the fact that I'd only recently moved to a particular part of the countryside near Stroud and my eyes were wide open at the beauty of what I saw, and I felt really compelled and driven and excited at the idea of finding the words for what I could see.

Q: One of the things that happens to Harold in the book is that he discovers the closeness of nature in a way which he had never understood before.

A: Yes—he had only ever seen it from a car, and I think it's extraordinarily exciting and liberating for him to be out there.

Q: It strikes you as a very natural male voice. I think it's about humanity, and the human mind and soul, rather than a male or a female character.

A: When I was writing it, I remember thinking I'm writing—I wouldn't say I'm writing an everyman, that seems a bit grandiose—an ordinary man. Sometimes you manage to tap into something when you write the ordinary. Not always, but I think Harold took me to a place where he somehow became bigger than himself, simply by being so ordinary.

Q: Is Harold suffering from a midlife crisis in the book?
A: Maureen thinks he's having a midlife crisis, but rather late. I don't think it is a midlife crisis as such—I think it's more of an existential crisis. But I think it's brought about by years and years and years of being asleep. He's got a point in his life and his marriage where it cannot go on with this stalemate, this isolation, this lockdown that he and Maureen are in. I think sometimes instinct kicks in, and it's not something he's thought about, but he has to become the person he truly is. He has to commit.

Q: One of the most moving and brutal lines in the book was: "as if he wasn't so much walking to Queenie as away from himself." Did Harold have to lose himself in the walk, literally without maps and even without a compass for most of it, in order to find a way to live again?
A: Yes, he does. He has to get lost in the woods. He has to go away from what is familiar, and it's only by doing that that he's able to let go of all these things that have held him back, and also that he's used as props to stop himself from looking at the things he doesn't want to see, which are his guilt, his fear, his loss, and his feelings of being completely incompetent.

Q: I see Harold as a decent man, but one who has failed to meet his own, and particularly others' hopes, in terms of the roles in life he's played: son, husband, father, friend. How much of the novel is about the expectations others have of us and the consequences of us not fulfilling them?

A: When I was writing it, I was thinking more about how important it is to learn how to express love, and that if you've been brought up as a child—as Harold has—in a place where no love is expressed or given, it's very hard to become a parent, but also a husband, and express what needs to be done, especially when your child is in trouble. Harold is not equipped—that's his tragedy—to say the things that need to be said. He's the kind of man my father was a little, who found it very hard to express emotions sometimes. There is no love in his life until he meets Maureen.

Q: Which brings us to Maureen, his wife, who is desperately unhappy, missing their son terribly, and there's a mystery attached to that. She plays a very important part because, although she is stuck there at home and Harold has gone off, she is really on a journey which is rather similar to his.

A: Yes, she's definitely on a journey, and of the two of them I find Maureen is almost the more moving. She doesn't ask to make that journey, and then she has to make it not out in the open where you have the stimulation of awakening to the world and awakening to other people—she has to do it all within the confines of her home.

Q: From the beginning of the book you made me believe in Harold; I loved his character and I willed him on his way on his walk. I didn't initially feel the same about Maureen; this belief in her developed at a much slower pace. Was this intentional in your writing? Did you want the reader to change their mind about Maureen once they got to know more about what she had been through?

A: Yes, I did. I feel that Maureen is one of those people who are more difficult to like initially, and that is very hard for her, especially when she sees Harold out in the world and looking so at ease with himself and quite handsome. But I think the other thing that's so hard for her is that she recognizes that she's a person who, even if she has something nice to say to Harold, by the time it gets to her mouth it's often not nice, she can't stop herself. So Maureen is a slow burn kind of character, and I always find it interesting if you take a character at the beginning who people don't necessarily warm to, and you reveal bit by bit why they've become the person who they've become. And actually, I find her a deeply sympathetic character that I'm constantly drawn back to, and in fact I'm writing about again now.

Q: The point of Harold's walk, his pilgrimage, is to get to Queenie with whom he used to work. We know that she is gravely ill. He could be interpreted as procrastinating his meeting with Queenie; we know early on that Queenie is in the hospice, and we get the sense her health at the start of the book is different from when we finally do meet her properly. It was frustrating that Harold took about three months to get to her, because obviously time was of the essence for her. What made you decide what Queenie's health was going to be like by the time Harold got to her, and were you tempted to write a version where Queenie was well enough to have a proper conversation with Harold?

A: I knew that I was going to write at some point from Queenie's perspective, so I wasn't too worried about giving her a voice in the book, and I knew that if we went too much with Queenie during the book I would destroy the tension of: What is happening with her? Will she be okay? But the other thing about Queenie, to be really honest, is that when I began writing the story as a radio play, it was because my father had just told us that he was dying, and I think it was probably, looking back, though I didn't see it at the time, my way of trying to cope and make beautiful something that was terrifying. So Queenie's cancer, the way that he finds her, is my dad's cancer, and I couldn't fudge that. So I knew that when he walked into the room, she wouldn't be able to speak and that for me, if I had allowed her to speak, and to have a conversation, it wouldn't have been true to what I knew.

Q: Through the character of Harold, readers were encouraged to explore the idea of the personal, or even the spiritual anguish, that some people go through when they know somebody, especially somebody who is closer to them, who is dying. In a society that rarely talks about such things, I thought this was really important. Since then, we've gone through a pandemic, and we as a society have been forced to think about death. Have you had any reflections on this anguish of being close to someone who's dying? Has the pandemic changed the way you think about your book? Do you think readers will react to it differently now?

A: In a way it's quite hard for me to talk about the effect the book has because I'm still so inside it, but I know that I thought a lot about isolation and I thought about people a lot during the first lockdown, certainly. I think of myself as a quite a lonely person in a good way, happy with being alone, but I realized how much I needed to come up against the unknown, and how unfocused I felt without it. I was lucky to have my family around, but I did think then about Harold and how I'd put him out in the world, and what you consciously know and unconsciously act on—they are linked.

Q: I found the novel one of great numinosity and quasi-religiosity, and yet none of the characters are conventionally religious. What were you really trying to say about the nature of faith and spirituality?

A: When I write a book, I think about a number of things. I really think about the story—how do I keep a person with me?—but there are normally also questions I want to ask, and one of them was very definitely: What is faith? If you don't go to church, which I don't. And what is a pilgrimage, now? I felt very strongly that Harold's journey is about putting himself out of the center of the picture, recognizing that you are part of something bigger and honoring it. It's a kind of surrender, and it's about the spirituality in nature or in other people—just recognizing that you are not "it." We are part of something much, much bigger, and we must honor it.

Q: You could say that Harold's journey was a journey of discovery, in all kinds of ways. It takes him 87 days to get from Devon to Berwick-upon-Tweed, and of course he's seeing different things, sampling different parts of the country. The geography of England almost acts like another character in his journey. What research did you do to get to know the specificity of the route, and how you were able to bring it to life so vividly?

A: I knew that if you don't have your facts straight, or at least appearing straight, readers smell it a mile off. So I did a lot of research; I actually stuck to a lot of places I knew. It just happens that Kingsbridge is where my husband was brought up, so I have a lot of clear pictures of Kingsbridge, and I have a strong affection for it. As he makes his way around the country, he actually sleeps in a barn in Stroud that I can see from my house in real life, and I went and practiced sitting on hay bales in it. A lot of it I used what I knew, but there did inevitably come bits where I was stuck. At one point I decided I needed a map, so I nicked the map from the car and started whipping out pages, and I just stuck it all over my wall. I had Kingsbridge, and then I worked my way up the country, and then I had this colossal map stuck to my wall. On a separate document, I knew where Harold sleeps—I'd even found his boarding houses—and it just got to the point where I thought, actually the reader doesn't need to know all this, but I knew. I think that's what's so exciting about fiction, that it combines research and then that other thing that we don't talk about so much, which is your imagination. Sometimes when I couldn't see the place, I used what I could see, and stepped slightly away. I found that really exciting.

Q: One of the things that happens to Harold is that he becomes an unlikely public figure because of this journey. The press and PR people in the book do not look good, and they use Harold's story because it happened to be a slow news day, and soon the press are making up stories about Harold, and PR people want to use him to sell drinks. Although this was quite humorous, it was a pity the press used Harold for their own benefit. Was there a reason why the press were not painted in a positive light?

A: I apologize to anyone who's in the press or publicity, obviously! But that bit of the book is a bit that really gets people, and a lot of people say, I just didn't like it when the pilgrims came along. And my answer is, you're not supposed to. It's not pleasant for anyone—it's not pleasant for Harold and it's not pleasant for the reader—but without that bit I felt that we would have remained in a bubble. Harold would have been in a bubble, and we'd have been in a bubble with him. It had to be broken, and he has to meet the collective. He has to meet a more cynical voice, and then he has to do what he has never done, which is to try and turn his back on it. It's a huge challenge for him, but he has to go through that, we have to go through that, in order for him then to deal with the biggest crisis that he deals with, which is the existential one as he's out on the heath.

Q: How did you decide to go ahead and write book more books about Queenie and Maureen? What made you sit down and actually do it?

A: As I was writing Harold and began to talk about the book and Queenie, I realized that it was actually three books, not one. But I didn't know if I had the strength to write all three. A couple of years after Harold Fry, I talked a lot about Harold and about Queenie, and I thought, well actually, Queenie isn't simply a woman in a bed dying, just as my dad wasn't just a man with cancer. So I felt very strongly it was the right time to write the Queenie book. It's now ten years later and I've written the last part, but it's taken me a very long time to feel ready.

Q: It's fascinating to hear you speak about your motivation for writing the book, and it seems to me that the process of *The Unlikely Pilgrimage of Harold Fry* is a kind of catharsis for you as well as for Harold, and for the reader.

A: Yes. I often think about what that book meant to me, and I now look back and think, throughout that story there's a search for forgiveness and it's not just Harold's, it's mine too. We all know it; when you lose a parent, when you lose someone you love, you carry this need to be forgiven that you couldn't save them.

Q: We've been talking about loss and grief, and there is tragedy hanging over this book in some ways, but it's also a very funny story. How did you decide to use laughter as a release instead of the typical emotions and actions associated with grief?

A: I'm always interested in that point where tragedy and comedy meet. It's a very rich place because of the conflict that it causes, but I also feel from my own experiences of grief that there have been moments of bonkers-ness around them. For instance, I was in a funeral cortege once, and we got stuck, literally all of us, down a dead end—we drove down a dead end. How ridiculously metaphorical, but not, is that? Life and grief,

I think, do not do the things that we might expect them to do or want them to do. And they're not always as solemn and serious as we want them to be. And I felt that Harold and Maureen deserved reckless laughter, and we're not really part of it. That was the other thing that was important to me—it's secret between them, we don't really know why they're laughing.

Q: But we almost want to close the curtain and let them enjoy it, don't we?

A: It's exactly that feeling—close the curtain, it's their story now.

AN EMAIL CORRESPONDENCE
WITH MAUREEN FRY

Dear Maureen Fry,

It has become a bit of a thing for me to add extra material to the end of a book, and I wondered if you would allow me to interview you?

With best wishes, Rachel Joyce

Dear Rachel Joyce,

Who are you? What book? And what do you mean by a bit of a thing?

Yours, Maureen Fry

PS Are you a journalist?

Dear Maureen Fry,

I am interested in asking a few questions by email but you are perfectly at liberty to refuse to answer them. I am not a journalist. I see myself as more of a very close neighbor.

Best wishes,

Rachel Joyce

Dear Rachel Joyce,

I am sorry. I still don't understand. Are you trying to speak to my husband?

Yours, Maureen Fry

PS Are you the neighbor who insisted on banging saucepans for the NHS during lockdown, even when the rest of us had stopped? Thereby disturbing the only person on our road who actually worked night shifts for the NHS?

Dear Maureen,

I am not.

Though I admit I did bang pots for a while. I didn't know what else to do. And I liked hearing everyone else bang theirs.

Best wishes, Rachel

Dear Rachel,

Yes. I confess I banged a few too.

All right. What kind of questions?

Maureen

Dear Maureen,

Questions that might help people understand a little more about you. For instance, are you a butter person, or a margarine person?

That kind of thing.

MF: *I do not eat margarine.*
You might as well not have toast.

RJ: Does this mean we are now having a conversation?
MF: *I am not sure. We'll see.*

On the whole, it seems to me that people want to know far too much about one another. And of course life isn't like that. It isn't that simple. There are people who photograph every meal they eat, and every cup of coffee, as if this will make them more transparent, when all it reveals is that they drink a lot of coffee.

RJ: Are you talking about social media?
MF: *My next-door neighbor recently discovered social media. He has five friends and one of them is a cat called Salisbury. Rex! I said. You are being followed by someone who pretends to be a pet. Rex seems happy, though. He posts pictures of birds so maybe I am wrong. Maybe he and Salisbury have a lot to offer one another.*

I suppose we all see things differently. And yet people seem less and less inclined to accept we are different, and therefore judge one another on their own terms.

I admit I have been judgemental myself in the past. It is hard to let go of prejudice and yet it is essential.

RJ: But do you value female friendship?

MF: I do not value anything simply for the sake of it. Do I value all friendships with women? No. I do not like all women, just as I do not dislike all men. As I get older, I feel less inclined to extend what I have, but instead to make more of what I know.

I am thinking again of my next-door neighbor, Rex. (Do you know this neighbor?) I realize he might not be an obvious choice for a friend but after years of smiling politely, and also lending him milk—when his wife died, he lost all ability to judge how much milk a person drinks—he became someone to whom I could tell almost anything. I could not say exactly how that happened, or why. Maybe it was simply a case of convenience, of us both being next door to one another at the same time we needed to say something.

Recently I met a woman who lived in a truck—actually she still lives in this truck. I misjudged her. The first time I saw her, with her hair in ribbons and her clothes more like a piece of sacking, I thought she looked made of wool. I assumed that because she lived in a certain way, i.e., in her truck, we had no common ground. It turns out I was wrong.

I realized through her that you can be with a person and not talk, and that is still a kind of conversation.

She and I now exchange cards regularly. I am planning to visit her again, though I have suggested we rent a small chalet by the sea, as opposed to her truck. You have to be on painkillers to think what she sleeps on is a comfortable bed.

RJ: Thank you, Maureen.

MF: I hope I didn't say too much.

RJ: I loved your answer.

MF: I have to say that the friendship question was better than the butter one.

RJ: It was intended as a warm-up. I agree it wasn't a very good one. I believe you are a keen gardener? Would you like to talk more about that?

MF: I have always grown plants that produce food. But I went on a trip recently. It was while I was on this trip that I met the woman I spoke of earlier, the woman who lived in a truck. I also visited a garden—and this may sound a small thing to you—but I do not know how to explain how this woman and this garden affected me. Did they change my life? No. But did they add to my way of thinking and being? Yes. It was through the strange language of this garden that I understood the limitations of myself.

Since making that trip, I have introduced several flowering plants to our garden. We have sunflowers, for instance, that are taller than my husband and crash sideways on a regular basis. My friend Kate sent me some seeds for my birthday. I wept. They were such vast flowers! And not remotely edible.

My husband says I have green fingers, which is very sweet of him, but really he is just amazed that things keep coming back, year after year. I didn't see the point in flowers until I met my friend Kate and visited Queenie's garden. Now I look at the flowers and I see Kate and Queenie too.

RJ: Can I ask more about Queenie?

MF: No.

MF (a day later): I wish I had been kinder to Queenie but we met at a time in my life when I could not be kind.

After my trip, a young man got in touch with me. He had been one of Queenie's carers when she was living beside her garden—he had driven her to the hospice where she spent the remainder of her life. He was racked, he told me, with guilt because he never visited her after that. It was too painful.

You see. We cannot always be the people we would like to be. But we can learn.

RJ: Was that a young man called Simon? He wore a duffel coat?
MF: It is. He now writes to Harold. How do you know Simon?

RJ: It's a long story.

Did the trip change you in any other way? Did it, for instance, change your attitude to reading?
MF: My mother once saw me with a book and asked if I hadn't anything proper to do. I was a young woman but it is hard to unpick that kind of thing. I would still prefer to be doing something rather than reading. That is not a judgment on reading; it is more a judgment on the kind of baggage we inherit.

RJ: Have you been back to your local bookshop since your journey? Do you still prefer to shop online?
MF: I have been back to my local bookshop. I bought ten postcards and also a keyring for my friend, Kate. I said hello to the owner. She asked how I was. We left it there. There is a danger in grief

just as there is a danger in happiness. If we do not have both, it is hard to feel empathy. I spent a long time without happiness.

RJ: What is your most treasured possession?
MF: My wedding ring.

RJ: Do you ever join your husband and Rex in their bird-watching?
MF: I make them sandwiches. My husband and Rex, not the birds. Though I suspect half the sandwiches go to the birds.

RJ: What advice would you give to a young woman today?
MF: Learn to play football.

RJ: Is there anything else you would like me to ask? Anything you feel I've missed?
MF: Would you follow my neighbor Rex on Instagram?

RJ: Of course I will. I will also follow the cat.
My last question. What do you think of the cover of your book? I have to say I love it.
MF: Book? What book?

QUESTIONS AND TOPICS
FOR DISCUSSION

1. Did you read *The Unlikely Pilgrimage of Harold Fry* or *The Love Song of Miss Queenie Hennessy* before reading *Maureen*? If so, what was your impression of Maureen from those books? Did it change upon hearing her tell her story here? And if not, what did you think of her character after being introduced to her in this book?

2. How has Harold's pilgrimage affected Maureen? How do you think that has affected her decision to make her own journey now? Are her motivations similar to Harold's? Why or why not?

3. While on her journey, Maureen reflects on how much has changed in the world over the last ten years: "En-

gland was a different country ... These days it was all
safe motorways and Uber. It was paying with your
phone, and please keep your distance, not to mention
podcasts, milk made of oats and meat made of plants,
and everything streamed online." How have you experienced change in your life, or in the world? Did you re-
late to her sense of displacement?

4. Do you think Maureen was justified in her opinions of
   Queenie? If you've read the other Harold Fry books, did
   this line up with your impression of Queenie as a character?

5. What did you imagine Queenie's garden to look like?
   How did you feel when you saw it through Maureen's
   eyes? Have you ever encountered anywhere similar?

6. What did you think of the driftwood that represents
   David? If you were to honor a loved one in Queenie's
   garden, what would you use?

7. How has Maureen's experience of grief for David
   shaped her life? In what way is that similar to, or different from, the way Harold expresses his grief?

8. What did you make of Maureen's encounter with Kate,
   from her first impression to her stay in the caravan?
   Have you had similar experiences with people? What
   does Maureen learn from her time with Kate?

9. How did you understand David's phrase "I am the world's guest"? Have you felt similarly in your own life?

10. Do you think anything changed in Maureen and Harold's relationship after she got back from her journey? What do you think it meant to both of them?

11. Is there a journey you've made in your own life that felt similar to Maureen's, either physically or spiritually? What did it mean to you?

RACHEL JOYCE is the author of the *Sunday Times* and international bestsellers *The Unlikely Pilgrimage of Harold Fry* and *The Love Song of Miss Queenie Hennessy*. *Maureen* completes this trilogy. She is also the author of bestsellers *Perfect*, *The Music Shop*, *Miss Benson's Beetle* and a collection of interlinked short stories, *A Snow Garden and Other Stories*. Her books have sold over five million copies worldwide and been translated into thirty-six languages.

The Unlikely Pilgrimage of Harold Fry was shortlisted for the Commonwealth Book Prize and longlisted for the Man Booker Prize. It is now a major film starring Jim Broadbent, with Penelope Wilton as Maureen. Rachel was awarded the Specsavers National Book Awards New Writer of the Year in 2012 and shortlisted for the UK Author of the Year award in 2014.

Rachel Joyce lives with her husband, Paul, and family near Stroud.

rachel-joyce.co.uk
Facebook.com/RachelJoyceAuthor
Instagram: @rachelcjoyce

ABOUT THE TYPE

This book was set in Caslon, a typeface first designed in 1722 by William Caslon (1692–1766). Its widespread use by most English printers in the early eighteenth century soon supplanted the Dutch typefaces that had formerly prevailed. The roman is considered a "work-horse" typeface due to its pleasant, open appearance, while the italic is exceedingly decorative.